Mary
Margaret Mary
Christmas

Mary Margaret Mary Christmas

by Christine Kole MacLean

*Dutton
Children's
Books*

DUTTON CHILDREN'S BOOKS
A division of Penguin Young Readers Group
Published by the Penguin Group
Penguin Group (USA) Inc., 375 Hudson Street, New York, New York 10014,
U.S.A. • Penguin Group (Canada), 90 Eglinton Avenue East, Suite 700,
Toronto, Ontario, Canada M4P 2Y3 (a division of Pearson Penguin Canada
Inc.) • Penguin Books Ltd, 80 Strand, London WC2R 0RL, England
Penguin Ireland, 25 St Stephen's Green, Dublin 2, Ireland (a division of
Penguin Books Ltd) • Penguin Group (Australia), 250 Camberwell Road,
Camberwell, Victoria 3124, Australia (a division of Pearson Australia Group
Pty Ltd) • Penguin Books India Pvt Ltd, 11 Community Centre, Panchsheel
Park, New Delhi - 110 017, India • Penguin Group (NZ), 67 Apollo Drive,
Rosedale, North Shore 0632, New Zealand (a division of Pearson New Zea-
land Ltd.) • Penguin Books (South Africa) (Pty) Ltd, 24 Sturdee Avenue,
Rosebank, Johannesburg 2196, South Africa
Penguin Books Ltd, Registered Offices:
80 Strand, London WC2R 0RL, England

This book is a work of fiction. Names, characters, places, and incidents are
either the product of the author's imagination or are used fictitiously, and
any resemblance to actual persons, living or dead, business establishments,
events, or locales is entirely coincidental.

Copyright © 2008 by Christine Kole MacLean

CIP Data is available.

Published in the United States by Dutton Children's Books,
a division of Penguin Young Readers Group
345 Hudson Street, New York, New York 10014
www.penguin.com/youngreaders

Designed by IRENE VANDERVOORT

Printed in USA   First Edition

ISBN 978-0-525-47973-4
1 3 5 7 9 10 8 6 4 2

For Hope
(She knows why)

Acknowledgments

Caroline McKnight and Ian McKnight named names for me,
Gordon Wiersma pondered forgiveness with me, Madeline
and Clark gave suggestions to me, and the fourth
graders in Mr. Schaap's class at East K-8 in Holland,
Michigan, included me. I'd like to thank them all.
Special thanks to my editor, Stephanie Owens Lurie, and
Dan Lazar.

Contents

Mary Margaret Mary Christmas

1. Up a Tree

I thought this time would never get here. The time school was over. The time my bus squeaked its squeaky-stop squeak at the end of my street. The time Rita, the bus driver, would say, "Don't be a pest, Celeste."

She always pretends she doesn't know our names. Molly, who is only five, falls for it every time. Rita will say, "Until we meet, Pete," and then Molly will say, all serious, "Hey, my name is MOLLY." But not me. I just give it right back to Rita. I say, "See you in the mornin', Lauren."

The doors *fwap* open in front of me. A pretend Rudolph is guarding the Kalinskis' house, right where he was when I got on the bus. His red nose beams off and on. He's probably been trying to make friends with the giant blow-up Frosty in Jolene's yard. Or he's been wondering why the plastic Santa across the street isn't coming over. Every house has a big Christmas decoration out front except ours.

And suddenly I remember why I couldn't wait for this time to get here. As soon as I get home, we are going to get our Christmas tree and it's MY year to pick the tree. All on my very own. Whichever tree I want.

I feel Mr. Mischief sneaking up in me and he sneaks right to my feet, which jump from the top step all the way down into the snow, and I don't even fall to my knees.

"Mary Margaret!" Rita says. "You know that'll get both of us in trouble. What are you thinking?"

Here is what I am thinking: It's a great day to be me! I grin up at her. "Made you say it! Made you say my name." And then I hop up and scamper away from there.

Inside the house, I drop my backpack and kick off my boots. "I'm ready!" I yell. "I'm ready to go find the best tree ever!"

"Hello to you, too, Mary Margaret," my mom says. She's in the kitchen feeding my baby sister, Eliza. My mom used to be just an ordinary mom, but a little while ago she had Liza. Now she is mush, which you can't see from the outside, but she is. Here is proof of that. When she was pregnant with Eliza (before we knew it was Eliza), my dad asked her what she wanted for Christmas and she said having a healthy baby was enough for her. This does not make sense. One, Liza did not come from a store, and she might be new, but she is not shiny or even attractionable. A new toy is hard to stay away from, but you *want* to stay away from Liza. Two, she has a very loud cry, which she uses whenever she feels like, even when it's not appropriate. And she does not have an on/off switch. There are other reasons, but I can't think of them right now.

My mom wipes Liza's mouth. "How was your day?"

"Plain. It was just a plain old day," I say. "Where's Dad?"

"He and JT are in the garage, getting the van ready," she says.

"Great! Let's go, let's go, let's go!"

"In a minute." She holds Liza out to me. "Would you burp her?"

I wrinkle up my nose. I'm the best burper in the family, which I feel sorry about because it means I get stuck doing it all the time. "No thanks."

"That's not very productive," she says.

Productive is her new favorite word. My dad told me it means helpful, useful, or positive. Her old favorite word is *exhausted*.

I shrug. "I want to work on my Christmas list."

"We'll be able to leave sooner if you do," my mom says.

Usually my mind in my head is strong, but sometimes my mom gets in there and paws around and changes my mind. Like now. I take Liza and pat her back, bottom to top, because that's the way to get the bubbles out. I'm so good at it I don't even have to look at Liza. So I watch my mom instead.

Pat-pat-pat.

My mom makes a bottle. "One for the road," she says, and drops it into the bag.

Pat-pat-pat.

"Oh! I know," she says. She runs upstairs without saying what she knows.

I wriggle Liza into carrying position and walk us over to the fridge, where my Christmas list is hanging. When I wrote my list, right after Halloween, at first I was going to tape it to my mom's bed, because she's in there all night. But when JT saw what I was doing, he said, "Yeah, but the whole time she's in there, she's *sleeping*."

"So?" I said, because I couldn't think of anything else to say right then.

"If her eyes are closed—which they are when she sleeps—then she isn't reading your list."

A few days later, I moved my list to the fridge.

Now I go to the bottom of page three and write *Buckin' Buckskin horse sheets (and also pillowcases)* right under *talking monkey—NOT REAL*.

My mom comes back with three diapers and a red-and-white shirt and blue stretchy pants for Liza. "Just in case," she says.

"I added Buckin' Buckskin sheets to my list," I say.

"Another present," my mom says, like she is not at all surprised.

"I just want to give Santa lots of choices."

"In case the elves are out of your top hundred things?"

"Right," I say.

She tucks the clothes and diapers into the bag. "Santa is old," she says. "He's going to take one look at all those ideas and give up. You'll end up with a lump of coal."

Hmmmm. I had not thought of that.

Uurrrrp, goes Liza.

"Yay!" I say. "Now we can go."

Mom frowns at Liza. "She's not done yet. Keep going."

I sigh and start my hand up again. *Pat-pat-pat.*

Mom opens and closes all the pockets in the diaper bag. "Out of wipes," she says. "I think there might be extras in the van. Oh! Her favorite chew toy. Let me think. Where did I see that?" She wanders out of the kitchen.

Here is the third reason Liza is not a present. Last year when we went to get a tree, it took about a minute for me, my brother JT, Mom, and Dad to get ready to go. Even though I was only eight way back then, I could do everything myself. And JT is thirteen and has been doing everything for a long time and even helping me sometimes. But ever since Liza came, it takes us seventy-six minutes. Sometimes longer.

Finally, Liza burps enough and my mom finds the chew toy. Mom zips Liza into her sleeping-bag-thingy. Liza screams. She hates that thing.

"Just think," my mom says, shaking her head. "Last year when we did this, we didn't even have Liza. We didn't even know there would be a Liza."

"Yeah," I say. "Those were the good old days."

On the drive to the Christmas-tree farm, Liza finally gives up on crying and falls asleep. I think about what my mom said about Santa and my Christmas list. What if she's right? My dad told me once that my mom is a distant relation of Santa, so maybe their brains work the same way.

"Mom, do you really think Santa would give up on me?"

Dad cranks his head around from the passenger seat beside Mom, who always drives. "Why would he do that?" he asks.

"Oh, we were talking about her long-ish list," my mom says. "He wouldn't give up on you, Loverly. It's just you say you want so many things. How can he know which things you really want? For that matter, how can any of the rest of us know?"

"She's right," JT says. "By the time I read to the end of your list, I forgot what was at the beginning. It's kind of like when Mom says, 'Feed Hershey and finish your home-work,' and before you're done with those things she says, 'Make the dinner salads, pour the milk, bring in the mail.' And you tell her not to pile it on."

"Because I can't keep it all straight."

"Right," says JT. "I can't even read through your list without you pushing me aside to add something new."

"I don't do that."

"Remember on Monday when I was standing there drinking milk, waiting for Mom to get off the phone? You added number thirty-eight."

"Only because I saw a Clever Heifer ad on TV. I had to add it to my list before I forgot I wanted it." That heifer tells you what's going to happen to you. You ask it a question like, "On my first day as a lion tamer, will the lions gobble me up?" and then shake the heifer until it moos. When you turn it upside down, you get the answer. That's one useful toy. Because if you're going to be a lion tamer, it's good to know ahead of time if you're going to get gobbled.

Mom, Dad, and JT all take turns looking at each other. Which means . . . something, but I don't know what.

Finally, JT says, "It's too much information, KWIM?" KWIM is code for "know what I mean." He must know that I don't really know what he means because then he says, "Your list gets all muddled and I can't remember anything that's on it. You should just put the things you *really* want on your list."

"I do really want all those things."

"Forget it," JT says. "You're hopeless."

But now the worry spikes up in me. "Dad, can you remember anything?"

My dad tugs on his baseball cap, which means he's thinking. After a minute, he says, "Nope. I got nothing."

My dad is a big kidder. He might be kidding. But what if he isn't? What if Mom and Dad can't remember anything I want—and neither can Santa?

I get very quiet. I don't want to make my list shorter. All those things on my list—everything from number one (handcuffs) to number fifty-seven (sheets) are things I really do want.

After a while, I remember something. I remember that things stick in your head when you sing them. Like when I wanted a dog for my birthday, and I changed the words to "Rudolph the Red-Nosed Reindeer" to help my mom see how much I wanted a dog. That didn't work so well that time—I got Hershey, a rabbit, instead—but maybe this time it will work. You never know.

So in my head I make up some new words to "Jingle Bells." I start with the verse.

This is what I want
For Christmastime this year
A rock music CD
So Liza I won't hear.
A puppy of my own
Please don't forget the bone
A Breyer horse and barn of course
And ship them to my home.

Then I write the part everyone knows how to sing—the "Jingle bells, jingle bells, jingle all the way" part. I decide to use it to remind Santa and everyone of how good I've been. There are lots of things I want for Christmas, but a lump of coal is not one of them.

Oh, I've set the table
When I was able
Been nice to Jolene
Cheered JT
Cleaned up pee
Never acted me-ean.
I make my bed
See Hershey's fed
Make sure I'm not bored
I never curse, I could be worse
And that's worth a reward!

After I'm sure the words fit the tune, I sing the song for my family. I sing it again. Then I say, "Come on! Sing it with me. I know you want to!" Mom and Dad do, but JT just rolls his eyes, like he's too cool for school. Or too hip for hop, which is a little saying I made up while I was playing with Hershey once.

By the time I'm done teaching them the song, we're at the tree farm. We get there at the best time because they're loading up the wagon to take people out to the tree fields.

"All aboard who's getting aboard," shouts the tractor driver. He looks back at us and grins. I lean against my dad and sigh with glad happiness. We get the same tractor driver every year, and every year he says the same thing. It is one of the true joys of Christmas.

The ride is bumpy, and my dad puts his arm around me so I don't bump right off the wagon. "What kind of tree are you going to pick?" my mom asks. "Douglas firs always smell so good!"

"Maybe. I know what I want it to look like."

"Just don't choose one with a white ribbon," she says.

"Why not?"

"Too expensive," she says. "There is no reason we should pay that kind of money for a tree."

"Unless it's perfect," says my dad.

"Not even if it's perfect," she says. "Business is down. We need to watch our spending, not go overboard."

"Relax. It'll pick back up again."

"This should be my busiest time of the year. What do

companies do over the holidays? They throw parties." My mom helps companies throw parties—and she gets paid for it. Which sounds like the best job ever. If everything goes straight, it is. But if things go a little crooked, she gets blamed. "And if my clients are cutting back, that means the Andersons need to cut back, too."

Uh-oh, I think. That means us.

"Just don't overreact," my dad says. Good old dad. But the rest of the ride is very quiet.

When we get to the Douglas firs, I don't even have to get off the wagon to know this kind of tree isn't right for me. "Nope," I say.

"But you haven't even looked," JT says. A Douglas fir is what JT picked when it was his turn.

"I can just tell this kind isn't right. The branches are too close together." JT frowns, but he knows rules are rules. And the rule is I get to decide and what everyone else thinks doesn't matter.

"White pines!" shouts the driver at the next section.

"Mighty fine!" we all say with him. Even the other people on the wagon say it. They must come here every year, too.

Dad, Mom, and JT all watch to see what I'll do. I jump off the wagon, and they follow, looking happy. We tromp around for a while. Dad and Mom take turns lugging Liza's carrier. Liza was still asleep when we got to the farm, and we all want her to stay that way.

We gather in front of lots of different trees. One is too tall. Another is too wide. And I don't like any of them anyway.

Finally, my dad lets out a holler and we all snowplow our boots right over to where he's standing. "I've found it!" my dad says, shaking the snow off a branch. "It's great! Good shape. Not too tall."

My mom nods in agreement. JT shrugs like it's okay with him, too.

I pretend to think about it, even though I know it's not the tree for me. I waggle my head. "Nope."

The tractor and wagon have already left, so we have to walk to the next section. Liza starts to fuss. But even that can't spoil my mood. I skip and jump ahead of everyone else, looking for fresh snow that I can leave my footprints in. I can tell that people are losing their Christmas spirit. It's a good thing I have enough for all of us.

"Scotch pine," announces JT when we get there.

"One of a kind!" I say, very cheerful, because that's what the tractor-driver man always says. But this time no one says it with me.

"This one is perfect," my mom says, stumbling over to the first one she sees.

"It has too many branches and they go all the way down to the ground," I say.

"It's a *tree!*" they all say together, like it's something that the tractor-driver man says every year.

"It's *supposed* to have a lot of branches," says my dad.

Liza turns up the volume, and I can tell by my dad's frown that he's getting ready to say that they've "had it." I have never heard my father say he's "had it" while tree shopping, but if I don't pick a tree soon, then he might throw the rules out the window and pick one himself. Happily, my giant lucky pig ear is in my coat pocket. I use it a lot at school, like when I want to be first in line, which is most of the time. Even though the ear is plastic, not real, it still works pretty good if I stroke it the right way—with my thumb, from the pointy tip all the way down the outside edge. And then start at the tip again. Rubbing it up *and* down doesn't work at all.

When the tractor driver comes back, my mom is sitting on the ground, trying to get Liza to SU (code for "shut up," which we are not allowed to say), and JT is looking at me like he wants to kill me or worse. I rub my pig ear faster.

"What—no tree?" the tractor driver asks. "Maybe I can help you. What is it you're looking for?"

"Good luck with that one. That's what *we're* trying to figure out," says JT. "Apparently your trees have too many branches."

The driver looks at me. "Really?"

"Maybe not too many. But they are in the wrong place. Where are the kind of trees that don't have branches around the bottom?"

His eyes light up. "Oh, sure, *those* trees," he says. "That's the variety most popular with kids. I can make any tree you pick out one of those trees with a very special tool I have. It's called the Room-for-Presents-Maker 2000."

Sighing with relief, I pat my pig ear. Everybody needs a lucky pig ear. But you can't get one just anywhere. You have to win it at the fair, like I did.

By the time the tree man trims the bottom branches off

our blue spruce tree and helps us tie it to our van, we're all pretty tired. JT is rolling his eyes around in his head like they are marbles or something, trying to show me how dumb it was to want a tree for how many presents can fit under it.

But later, I hear JT humming "Jingle Bells," and I'm pretty sure he's remembering my words to the tune. Which means he's remembering what I want for Christmas. So maybe Mom and Dad and Santa will, too. My mood is all light and free because of that. Until my mom, who has been very quiet, says, "I think we all need to remember there is more to Christmas than presents."

That's what grown-ups think.

They're wrong.

Firstly, at Christmas, everyone shops. Which is about PRESENTS. Secondly, what do Santa and the elves do? They make and deliver PRESENTS. And commercials on TV do not say anything about peace and goodwill. They are about PRESENTS. The short way of writing Christmas is Xmas, and X always marks the spot. It marks the spot where the PRESENTS are. Lastly, Baby Jesus got presents. The men who came were called WISE men because they knew Christmas was about presents.

But I do not say any of that, otherwise my mom will try to climb into my head and change my mind. And me and my mind like us just the way we are on the topic of Christmas and presents.

2. Names Will Never Hurt Me

Mary
Margaret
Mary

At school the next day, there is a clump of kids around Mr. Mooney's desk. I pretend I'm a snake and slither my way through the clump until I get to Hannah, who is square-ish and won't even let a snake like me slither by. So I switch to pretending I'm a billy goat and give her a butt with my head. Finally, I get to the front. Where I belong.

Right between his dictionary and a sign that says PLEASE DON'T TOUCH is a fantastical snow globe. Inside it four tiny people ride in a tiny red sleigh. A black horse pulls them over a bridge and toward a house in the woods. And standing in the doorway of the house is a woman, holding up a lantern.

"She's lighting the way for them," says Ellie.

"So they don't get lost," says McKenzie.

"So they stop before getting to the dark woods," says Kyle.

"Yeah, to use the bathroom," says Noah, who I think of as Bathroom Boy, because he's always asking if he can go to the bathroom.

"It was handmade," says Mr. Mooney. "And here's the best part." He picks up the globe and gently shakes it. The snow drifts down onto the horse and sleigh. When he turns on a switch, a little light comes on in the lantern and music tinkles out. It's "Over the River and Through the Woods."

"My mom loves that song," I say. "We always sing it on the way to my grandpa's farm. Where'd you get it?"

"On eBay," says Mr. Mooney. "It's a rare find and one of a kind. I doubt you'd be able to find another like it."

The good news on that is I don't have to find it. That's Santa's job.

Mr. Mooney herds us back to our seats, and he tells us we'll all have a chance to make our own snow globes on Winter Workshop Day. I know from last year that Winter Workshop Day is when some nice ladies come in and help us make a present for our parents. Or, if you are unlucky and don't have Christmas or Hanukkah at your house, they help you make something you keep for yourself.

"Most of the things you need will be supplied," he says, "but everyone needs to bring in a clean jar. What kind of jar did I say you needed?" He cups his hand behind his ear and leans forward.

"A *cleeaan* jar," we all say together, very cooperative.

"That's right. It has to be clean. And if you have any special little trinket you want to put in, bring that along, too."

After Mr. Mooney swigs down some water, he says, "Now I want to tell you about a new assignment."

"You mean you're making us start something new *now*—right before Christmas?" wails Arial/Whopper Girl. She's this girl who tells the biggest whoppers I've ever heard. And then she acts like they are the truth. Which they are not. Once she said she met the President and his hand was sweaty when she shook it and then he offered her a piece of stale German chocolate cake. That's another thing about her lies. They have these details that make you think the lie might be true. That is why I call her Whopper Girl—because no one is better at lying than her. But I only call her that to myself. To her face, I call her Arial.

"My calendar says we still have plenty of time to do this project," Mr. Mooney says. "Just because it's December doesn't mean it's the holidays."

Holidays is code for "Christmas." But the teachers never call it Christmas because some people don't celebrate Christmas. Which I don't really understand, unless you get to celebrate Hanukkah instead, because if that's the holiday you pick, you get presents every day for a bunch of days in a row. When I heard that, I asked my mom if we could trade in Hanukkah for Christmas, but she said that wasn't the way it worked. Anyway, the teachers don't talk about Christmas, I guess because they don't want anyone to feel left out.

"We've studied the history of our land," he says. "We know all about the Native Americans and why the Pilgrims came to America. We are going to spend the rest of our time before holiday break talking about you."

This is fine for me. Me is my very favorite subject and something I know a lot about.

"Me?" asks Drew, pointing to himself. "We're going to spend all that time on me?"

"You'll be spending all that time on you. Your classmates will be spending that time on themselves. I thought up a little game to play, just to get ourselves in the groove. It's a memory game."

This is fine for me, too. I love games, especially when I win them.

"Let's go around the room and tell everyone our middle names," he says, passing out yellow cards. "Then for the rest of the morning, every time you talk to someone you must use his first and middle name. If you don't and he or she catches you, you must give him or her your card—and all the cards you've already collected from others. The person who has the most cards wins." He sighs like he's done talking but then says, "Oh, and one more thing. Parents choose a certain middle name for lots of different reasons—they like the name, or it's been in the family for a long time, or it's someone they admire. Other people's names might not make sense to us, but that's no reason to laugh at them. No comments from the peanut gallery—that would be you—when you hear a person's middle name, and that includes snorting or giggling."

He looks at us over his glasses for a long time. "Am I clear?"

I nod, very serious.

"Good. Mary Margaret? Let's begin with you."

I'm first because I sit in the front row. Mr. Mooney put me there after the first week of school because he likes me a lot. Also to make it easier to have "little talks" about my behavior. But I'm pretty sure it's mostly because he likes me a lot. Sitting in the front row means I automatically get to be first sometimes, which works out good for me. Except now.

"What's your middle name?"

That's when my brain ices. Because the true thing is I don't have a middle name. And since everyone already has the habit of calling me Mary Margaret all the time, I'll never get anyone's card and I won't win the game. Which I really want to do.

Then, all on its own, because my brain is still iced, my mouth says, "Mary."

A few kids gasp. I know what they mean, because I am shocked up, too—at my mouth.

And my mouth is not done yet. "I know it sounds weird," it says, "but my mom wanted to name me Mary Margaret but my dad wanted to name me Margaret Mary. So they named me Mary Margaret Mary Anderson." My head starts bobbing like crazy, like it agrees with my mouth. I wonder if my brain feels left out.

Mr. Mooney frowns down at me. "Hmmm," he says.

My brain finally has something to say, and it's *Wait! Wait! We didn't mean to say that!* But my mouth doesn't say it, and then it's too late.

Behind me Kyle is saying, "Robert."

Then Hannah says, "Louise."

And then I'm listening hard and repeating "Kyle Robert" and "Hannah Louise" and "McKenzie Alice" and all the other names as kids say them so I can win. What I'm not doing is I'm not thinking about what I said. And it wasn't so bad, anyway, because Mary *is* part of my name. I'm only making the game fair. Because that's what games are supposed to be.

At first we're all jangled up over the game. We talk slow and stumble over each other's names because we're all trying so hard to win. Then we do math, and by the time we get to reading circle, people are starting to forget. But not me. That's because I have a little trick up my shirt. And my trick is that I don't think about math or reading because those are what Mr. Mooney would call "distractions." Also, even when I just think about the person, I think about their first and middle names as all one name, just like Mary Margaret. So when Noah Alexander asks to go to the bathroom, I think, Oh, Noah *Alexander* is going to the bathroom. That's how his middle name makes a new tunnel into my brain.

Kyle is the first one to lose his card. "Here, Mary Margaret," he says, handing me his yellow card. He smiles big at me.

"Kyle Robert," I say. "You owe me a card."

"I know," he says, staring at the card he's already holding out to me. "Here it is."

"Got you! I got you!" I sing. I turn around. "Look, everybody! I got Kyle Robert's card."

Kyle Robert scowls at me. "Only because I wanted it to be over with."

I don't believe him. Who wants to quit a game? "You're just saying that."

"No, I'm not! I don't like to play games. I wanted you to get my card, not anyone else." He kicks the leg of the table. "But now I wish I picked someone else."

Then a lightbulb goes off in my head. "Oh, now I get it," I whisper to Kyle Robert. "You just don't want to be laughed at for losing so early."

"Kyle Robert *wanted* me to have his card," I announce. Then I smile at him like a tricky fox. Kyle Robert stomp-stomps away. I don't really get what he's mad about. I was only helping him.

And now that I have his card, I have other things to think about. Like how to get everyone else's.

Pretty soon I can tell that McKenzie Alice has a trick up her shirt, too. But her trick is to win by not talking to anyone. "McKenzie Alice, you have to talk," I announce very loud. "Or none of us will talk to you." When she still doesn't talk, no one talks to her, thanks to me.

I get a few more cards from kids who are sucked into their reading so much that when I ask them a question, they forget all about the game. Especially if you ask a question like when cows laugh, does milk come out their nose? Which I ask my friend Ellie Paige. "I don't know, Mary Margaret," she says. She slaps her hand over her mouth, but then she knows it's too late and she laughs because she knows games are for fun.

Or if you just keep leaning over someone who is trying to read. Especially if you sigh and maybe whisper "meow" or "quack." Which is what I do to Ethan Liptor.

I have to lean and sigh for a long time, but finally he swats at me and says, "Mary Margaret, quit bugging me!"

Or if you tell a joke. "Why did the dog cross the road?" I ask Tristan Percival.

"Oh! Oh! My dad told me this one," he says. "It's because his leash ran out. Get it?"

"No."

"Leasing is like renting an apartment. The dog's *lease* ran out. Get it? Leash, lease! He didn't have a place to live. That's why he crossed the street. He was going to look for someplace to live, maybe a bigger place with a view, or three bedrooms, or a pool for all his doggy friends to swim in, or maybe—"

"Oh, *never mind!*" I say, kind of loud, because the right answer to the joke is "To get to the barking lot," but Tristan Percival messed it up with his own answer and it didn't seem like he was going to say my name, anyway. I look around for someone easier.

That's when Mr. Mooney says from the back of the room, "Your schoolwork should not be suffering from this game—nor should anyone else's. If you can't exercise some self-control, you will forfeit your cards." I do not look at him. I already know he is looking at me. "That means you, Mary Margaret."

Too bad he's not playing the game, otherwise I'd have another card.

I exercise some self-control. Until recess.

Lauren Ashley is sitting on the swings, so I go up and say, "What're you doing?"

"Just thinking about Christmas," she says. "I hope I get what I really want—a trip to Antarctica, where there are lots of penguins and no people. I can't wait to find out what I'm getting!"

"I could find out what I'm getting if I wanted," I say. Her mouth pops open and she stares at me. "It's a true thing. Because when my mom got back from Christmas shopping last week, she carried a We B Toys bag into her bedroom. And then later she said, 'Mary Margaret, will you go get my slippers by my bed?' And while I was in there, I saw the edge of the bag sticking out from underneath a pile of dirty clothes!"

"Wow, Mary Margaret. And you didn't even look?"

"No, I did not," I say, all proud. I'm proud I did not look (yet), but right then I'm more proud because I made her say Mary Margaret without the extra Mary. "And I'll take your yellow card now."

"It's not fair!" she says. She looks like she might cry. "This is recess!"

"So? That doesn't mean the game is on pause. You got any others?"

She turns over the one she won from Jacob Xavier plus the one *he* won from Caleb Stone.

I climb to the top of the thing we all call the castle and yell, "Attention, Mr. Mooney's class. I'm W-I-N-I-N-G!"

"Only because your name is so D-U-M!" someone yells. But I can't see who.

A few minutes later, when I'm pretending to be a horse and galloping along the fence, McKenzie Alice catches up to me.

"You're not winning, Mar—*you*," she says, changing her mind about using my name at the very last second. She's too scared she'll lose her card to me. "Someone else has more than you already."

"Who?"

McKenzie Alice presses her lips together hard and shakes her head. Which looks pretty dumb, the way she is hallumphing beside me, trying to keep up.

"If you aren't going to tell me, why'd you even come over here?"

Finally, she unzips her lips enough to say, "Because you have a big head and it needed to be shrunked."

"At least I don't gallop like a Heffalump," I say.

"You—you—you think you're so special, Mary Margaret," she says.

"Ha-ha, McKenzie Alice," I tra-la-la as I stop my horse and put out my hand. "You owe me your yellow card." She just sits there, so I snap my fingers because I have got to finish riding the range before the end of recess.

She finally hands over the card. "But you are not nice."

"I am, too. I say please and thank you. And I help out with stuff."

"You're braggy. But you know what? You're not special at all. You're just . . . *average*."

When I hear her say that, I feel like my pretend horse's legs turn to wet noodles, and him and me *thunk* down into the dirt. It's a thunk that jolts through my guts and my heart and maybe my liver, even though I'm not sure where my liver is, exactly. It's definitely not an *average* thunk. And that cheers me up a little. I kick my horse up out of the dirt, and myself, too.

"Well, you're just a sore loser," I say. My mom says calling people names is not very productive or useful. But calling McKenzie Alice a sore loser makes me feel better. And that is useful to me.

Then me and my speedy steed spin around and leave her and her laggy nag behind. While I'm looking back to see just how far behind, me and my horse crash right into Hannah Louise and bounce off her like she's a big rubber ball. And then I really do fall down.

I rub my shoulder. "Owww. You should get out of the way when you see a horse and rider coming."

"I didn't see a horse and rider coming," she says. Her pretending skills are low-ish, which makes me feel kind of bad for her. Because pretending sparks up life a lot. She puts out her hand to reel me up off the ground. "My sister says she is going out with your brother."

"Going out where?"

"You know—*going out with*. It means holding hands and kissing and stuff."

JT hates anything gross, which kissing definitely is. "JT wouldn't get mixed in with a girl," I say.

"Nope," she says. "They are. Ask him. Natalie thinks he's *splendid*."

I wrinkle my nose up. "Splendid?" JT is skinny and he's not ugly or anything, but he's not splendid. "Are you sure it's *my* JT?"

"Yup," she says. "Only now it looks like he's Natalie's JT."

3. Lips and Lipizzaners

Wait!" my mom says. "I just finished mopping that floor."

I take my hand off the laundry-room door. "I can't find my fringed pants and I think they might be in there," I say.

And then my mother does a shocker. She puts Liza in her playpen and says, "I will find them for you." My mother is always telling us to find things for ourselves because she is not going to come to college with us just so she can help us find socks, an overdue library book, or the goldfish. So she is not herself today.

She finds them hanging on the back of the bathroom door. "They must have walked themselves right over there," I say.

"Right, and climbed up to the hook," she says.

"They are special pants, must be."

"Must be." She sits down on the chair next to me. "Hey, I have some happy news for you. The tickets to the Lipizzaner show came today."

"You mean the World Famous Lipizzaner Stallions

Show?" I say. Mr. Mooney says that if you call something by its official name, that means you respect and admire it. And I sure do admire those big white horses prancing and leaping and frisking. And they do all of it *in the air*!

"Yes, the World Famous Lipizzaner Stallions Show."

"Eek!" I squeak. Because horses are one of my very favorite things, along with dogs. And, depending on my mood, a few other animals. But mostly horses and dogs.

"We're going during Christmas break," says my mom. "Remember—character is the ticket."

"Character is the ticket" is a shortcut so my mom and dad don't have to give me another long talk about how I did not do the right thing, which they kept giving me recently when I went through a "stretch of bad choices." That's what my dad called it.

First, I made Jolene, my neighbor who is five, empty the dishwasher before I would play dolls with her. Even though it seemed like a fair trade to me, because I don't like playing dolls and she doesn't like emptying the dishwasher. But my dad did not see things exactly that way. This is the way our talk went.

He said the dishwasher was my responsibility.

And I said, "I'm getting it done."

And he said, "No, you need to DO it. Not get someone else to do it." Which I thought was kind of picky.

A few days after that, there was a mix-up with me, my down comforter, scissors, glue, and Itzy, my friend Andy's dog. My mom told me that if I knew what was good for me, I should never talk about it again. (But if I could talk about it, I would just like to say down feathers and glue work better than snow when you are trying to make a snow-dog, because snow doesn't stick on a real dog. Also, Itzy thought it was fun.)

And that weekend . . . well, some other stuff happened in there, too.

My mom and dad gave me so many little talks that I got tired of them, and they got tired of them, too. So now we have a shortcut. "Character is the ticket" means for me to be the best person I know how to be. And if I have another attack of bad choices, then no World Famous Lipizzaner Stallions Show for me.

Which would be very sad.

"So how was your day?"

"Great. I won the name game." And then I explain all about how the game worked and how tricky I was—only I leave out the part about making up a middle name for myself, because it's not like I actually made up a name. I just repeated one of the names I already had.

I save the best part of the story, which is the very end, for last. "And then at the very end of the day, I got Elizabeth Kiera's cards—and she had a lot of cards because we all call her Kiera but that's actually her middle name, and her first name is Elizabeth, which hardly anyone could remember. Except me!"

"Good job," says my mom. "But you know I'd be proud of you even if you didn't win, right? The most important thing is that you play fair."

I nod.

When the phone rings and she gets up to answer it, I add on a silent gulp to my nod.

JT jogs through the kitchen, heading for the laundry room. Mom just about breaks a leg getting to the door first. "You can't go in there," she whispers. But at almost the very same time, she says into the phone, "New Year's Eve? Yes, I have that date available." She is good at multi-talking.

JT holds out his hands, which means, *Why not?*

And she pulls her eyebrows together, which means, *Just don't.*

Shooed away by Mom, JT sits down next to me. "What's new, Mary Magi?"

JT is always twisting my name around like it's a toy. Most of the time I don't mind, because I'm pretty sure he likes me way at the edges of his heart, even when he says I'm annoying. I wish I could give it right back to him, the way I do to Rita my bus driver, but so far I haven't figured out anything to do with J and T besides calling him J. Pee.

I would have told him about winning at school, except that all the happiness of that sizzled out of me when Mom mentioned that thing about playing fair. Plus JT is the one with something new.

"Nothing. What's new with *you?*" I say, knowing for real and for true what's new with him.

"Not much."

"That's not what Hannah Louise says."

"Who's Hannah Louise?"

"Hannah Louise *Heartwell*?" I say. "She has an older sister, *Natalie*? You know—the girl you're smooching it up with?"

"Shh-shh-shh!" he says, looking around for Mom. She's still zoned on the phone. "We are not smooching it up!" he hisses like a snake, leaning close to me so Mom won't hear. "And don't say anything in front of Mom."

"If you're not going with her, then why do you care?"

"Shh!" JT says. He gets up and waves at me to follow him into the living room. Which I do. Because this little talk is interesting. "I guess we are going together," he says. "But not kissing. Not that it's any of your business."

"But Hannah Louise says that's what *going with* means. You kiss and hold hands and stuff."

"That's not what it means to me," he says. "Is that what Natalie thinks it means?"

"Why don't you ask her?"

JT turns a little red at that idea. "We don't really talk, just say hi in the hall."

"Don't you do that with all girls?"

"I guess, except then Natalie's friend Taylor asked me if I liked Natalie. Natalie seems nice, so I said yes. The next day at lunch Taylor told everyone Natalie and I were going together."

"Why didn't you just say that you weren't?"

"Why do you think? Natalie was standing right there.

I don't have to do anything different. It's not a big deal, so don't make it into one. And don't talk about it—especially with her sister."

I hang my head and shake it like a sorrowful hound dog. I feel a little sorry for JT right then. And for me. "I can't believe it. Hannah Louise was right."

"Would you stop using both of her names?" JT says, like he is annoyed with me. But it's not my fault he is going with Natalie.

I am ready to be annoyed right back at him, but just then Mom comes in.

"What did you need from the laundry room?"

"My Toledo Mud Hens cap," he says.

"It's by the back door," she says. "Just don't—"

"Don't worry. I'll stay away from your precious just-mopped laundry-room floor."

But here is a funny thing. The laundry room wasn't just mopped. I know because I saw the mop in the garage. It was standing the way Mom puts it when it's dry. Another funny thing is my mom never talks to us when she is on the phone with a client. So there is something fishy about the laundry room. Or something very Christmassy. Like maybe there are presents in there. Presents that have not been wrapped yet.

Half of me wants to know what I'm getting for Christmas and half of me doesn't, because if I know, Christmas morning will be spoiled for me. So far, my good half has controlled me from digging through that dirty-clothes pile in Mom's room to find out what my present is. But now I know *two* hiding places of presents, and that means it will be double hard not to look.

For a girl like me, who is naturally curious, that's bigger than a problem. It's a trouble. And I am going to have to keep a double eye on myself.

4. I Give Myself a Present

'm doing my desk work, which is usually not number one on my list of best things. But Christmas is coming—at least to our house—and I know that Santa sees me when I'm sleeping, sees when I'm awake, knows if I've been bad or good, so I'm being good for goodness' sake.

Which is not that hard to do this time. Because the desk work is more like desk fun. We're supposed to write a poem about our family coming to America. Mr. Mooney calls it a creative exercise, and I've been exercising hard. So far, mine is like this:

In the year of 1492
Columbus sailed the sea of blue
To discover our America
With his white dog, Erica.

I'm putting a lot of thinking into what I should rhyme about next when a shadow shades my desk.

"I was right, huh?" It's Hannah Louise.

I tip my head back (way, way back) and look up at her.

"Going together doesn't mean kissing," I say. "It just means saying hi and feeling funny about it."

"But I was right about them going together."

I shrug because JT said not to talk to Hannah Louise about it.

"She likes the new polka dots," Hannah Louise says. "I like squares. They are neater."

"Oh," I say. Hannah Louise is not the easiest person to talk to. She says things in the wrong order sometimes or in a weird way, like "new polka dots." What makes the new ones different from the old ones? I don't know why she does it. Maybe it's because she doesn't practice talking that much.

But her mouth must be getting used to talking because she keeps going. "You should tell your brother. About the new polka dots."

My neck hurts from staring up at her. "Why?"

"It might help when he's buying her a present."

"Why would he buy her a present?"

"It's *Christmas* and they are *going together*. That's what people who go together do at Christmas. What does your brother like?"

Before I can answer, Mr. Mooney says, "Hannah, I don't see how talking to Mary Margaret is helping you get your writing done."

"Find out," she whispers to me. "My sister wants to know." And then she clumps back to her desk. She is a loud walker.

I read over my poem again.

In the year of 1492
Columbus sailed the sea of blue
To discover our America
With his white dog, Erica.

Then I add:

He brought that dog
He brought a pony
To the land
He would call home-y.

Already I think my poem is good enough to show Mr. Mooney, and so I do. And he says it's fine work except that it is not about the Pilgrims or the Andersons and to please go back to my desk and make the poem about the Pilgrims and the Anderson family, which is my family. I say okay, because poems burst out of me almost as fast as ideas.

Back at my desk I look in my book to remind myself what year the Pilgrims showed up here and then I write this:

In the year of 1620
Pilgrims found our land of plenty
They ached and moaned to be free
Just like we all want to be.

Anderson, big and strong,
Decided he would come along.

He cut and built
Then game he kilt.

He sent his wife and son
To make the hot-cross buns
And his spunky daughter
To fetch cool, fresh water.

She was kind and smart and good
As she skipped through the neighborhood.
When the settlers got ill
She gladly brought them pills.
And when they so sadly died
Mary Margaret for them cried.

Squanto showed them what to do
But she taught him a few things, too.
English songs and little poems
Everyone felt right at home.

And so the colonies were a hit
All thanks to Mary Margaret.

I think about adding Liza in, but that would ruin it. Loudmouth baby sisters do that. Ruin things even when you can't figure out exactly how they do it. So I leave her out.

I'm the first one done, which is a happiness.

"Mr. Mooney," I say, "I'm done with my poem about me and the Pilgrims."

Mr. Mooney says, "So soon?" but I can tell that he is not surprised. "Bring it up and put it in the workbasket."

When I'm walking back to my desk, I see Lauren Ashley's poem, which is very short. "You only have three lines done?" I say, very surprised. "But it's so easy!"

Lauren Ashley scowls, which I recently learned is one step worse than a frown.

"Not for everyone," Mr. Mooney says in a way that means I should zip my lip.

I zip it and hope like crazy Santa is busy watching somebody else right then.

Right before it's time to go home, Mr. Mooney tells us a special guest will be coming to talk to us in the morning. "Mr. Winthorp, Daisy's uncle and an expert on the Pilgrims, will tell us some new things about them. We're looking forward to it."

Daisy Ace lights up like a flashlight. "The stuff he knows is fascinating!" she says. "You know how the Pilgrims 'found' corn and etcetera?" She always adds that etcetera word to her sentences, maybe because it's fun to say. "Well, they found it on top of an Indian burial ground. They were grave robbers!"

Everybody gasps. Daisy Ace smiles and nods. "Yup, it's true. It was buried in the sand for the dead person's trip to the next life. And you know what else? That rock—the Plymouth Rock? Well, that didn't even—"

Mr. Mooney holds up his hand. "All right, Daisy. Let's leave something for your uncle to say tomorrow, shall we?"

"Okay, but it is so cool. You are going to love it. I can't WAIT!" she squeaks.

I can smell the chocolate-chip cookies almost before I open the door to our house. JT is already at the kitchen table, pouring milk. I drop my backpack and get myself a glass, too.

"Hey, Mary Miscreant," he says.

I pretend not to hear him, because I don't know what *miscreant* means, and besides it sounds like a made-up word to me.

I just say, "Where's Mom?"

"She went to get the flyers made up for her business so she can start mailing them and drum up some business."

"I hope it works." I look over at my list on the fridge that has all the things I really, really, really want and probably won't get if Mom doesn't get more work. Santa can only do so much. The rest is up to my mom and dad.

I research the plate of cookies, trying to figure out which ones have the most chocolate chips. When my hand is on its way to one cookie, it accidentally touches another one. A smaller one.

"That one's yours," JT says, all full of glee.

"No fair!"

"Sure it's fair. You know the rule. You touch it, you take it."

That is a dumb rule, but I take the stupid cookie and eat it. "I didn't mean to touch it," I say. Crumbs spill out of my mouth.

"Don't talk with your mouth full," he says.

I make a face at him, a face that means, *Don't tell me what to do.*

"I hear you told everyone you have a middle name, Mary Margaret *Mary*," he says.

I stop chewing. "How'd you know that?"

"Hannah told Natalie. Natalie told Taylor. Taylor told me."

"I just wanted to play the game. Besides, it wasn't like a Whopper Girl lie or anything," I say.

"Whopper Girl? Who's Whopper Girl?"

"Arial. She's a girl in our class who tells huge lies. Anyway, it's not one of those. It's just a white lie, like the one Mom said about having just mopped the laundry room. I saw the mop and it was dry."

"Oh! So there's . . ."

"Christmas presents in there," we both say together.

"There are also some in the bottom half of the linen closet—where all the extra blankets are," he says before I can stop him. I do not DO NOT want to hear where there are more presents hidden. But I don't even have time to think about that, because then he says, "If you don't tell Mom and Dad about that name-game thing, I will."

Here is a funny thing about JT. Sometimes he thinks he should be my parent—especially when a parent is not around to catch me when I mess up. This is very annoying. Two parents are enough for me. Usually I'd tell him to stop, but I don't want to get in a fight about that right now.

"JT, please don't. Please, please, please? Because if you

do, I won't be able to go see the World Famous Lipizzaner Stallions Show." It was just a little lie for fun and nothing bad happened because of it. But there is a chance that my dad will not see it that way. There is a chance he will think I'm still on my stretch of bad choices, even though I'm pretty sure I have gotten off that stretch.

JT chews on his thumbnail, which means he is thinking hard.

"Please?" I say again. Then I remember something that might help convince him. "I can tell you some stuff about Natalie."

He stops chewing his nail. "What about her?"

"Not until you promise not to tell."

He tibbles his fingers on the table. I can tell he is having a little talk with himself, trying to decide.

"It's really good stuff," I say.

He doesn't say anything.

Right then I think of something. "Be right back!" I say, and sprint out to the hall. I dive my hand into my coat pocket and give my lucky pig ear a quick stroke, from the pointy tip all the way down the outside edge. Then I run back to my chair and sit down.

JT frowns at me, so I worry that maybe I've worn out my lucky pig ear. But then he says, "Okay, but I'm telling you, Mary Margarine, you better stop stretching the truth—which is also known as lying."

I nod hard. "I will work on that—honest and for true."

"So what about Natalie?"

"She's getting you a Christmas present. Hannah

Louise told me. And she thinks you're getting her one!"

JT is so shocked up that he goes white. "A present? Wait. I have to buy her a present?"

"She likes polka dots," I say because I want to help him. "That's what Hannah Louise says."

"Isn't that whole name game over with?" he says, all annoyed. "And I thought I told you not to talk to Hannah Louise—*Hannah*—about Natalie."

"I didn't. SHE was talking to ME. I don't know why you're all of a sudden all mad at me. It's not my fault you're going with Natalie."

JT wads up his napkin and throws it as hard as he can. It floats to the floor in front of the stove. "It's just that . . . this whole girl thing is a mystery. Stuff happens and there's no way to even figure out how it happens, so then it happens again." When he leaves, he steps right over his napkin. I open my mouth to tell him he better come back and take care of his own trash, but then remember that he's not tattling on me, which is pretty nice, so I pick up the napkin for him and throw it away. As he stomps up the stairs, I hear him mumble, "Present? No way."

That reminds me that JT and me both have a present problem, and mine just got bigger. Because now, thanks to JT, I know three places in the house where there are presents waiting for me to find them. I could tell my parents I know where the presents are and to please move them. But that would mean I could never change my mind about snooping and I am the kind of girl who likes to leave all choices open. Especially at Christmas.

So I create a rule: Never be in the house by myself. Even for a few minutes. Because that will be too much for me. After all, I am only nine and haven't had that much practice at building up my "control yourself" muscle.

I go into my room to look for things for my snow globe. Already I know what my snow globe will be about. It will be about me. And I will give it to my mom and she will love it because the topic of it will be me.

I scrummage through the stuff on my desk until I find an old-fashioned jar my grandma used for peaches. It's perfect because it's big enough for my big idea.

In my jewelry box, I find my charm bracelet, which I never wear because it always gets in the way and can be dangerous, like if you're running a race and trip and fall on it just right, it could poke your eye out. And even when it's not poking my eye out, it's always poking my arm. So I don't wear it. It just sits there in my jewelry box. Which is not very productive. I take the horse and dog and heart charms off.

In my secret treasure chest, I find three small rubber fish and some tiny glitter stars and hearts.

Next I go looking for my very own miniature Nativity scene because I am going to need some of that for my snow globe. Usually a Nativity scene has a baby Jesus, who is the center of attention, Mary and Joseph (his exhausted parents), and a few wise men, shepherds, and animals. Also a big star and a stable. The only things I find are the stable, baby Jesus in his manger, and a wise man and a shepherd. But I'm pretty sure I can make my idea work.

After I have that all settled, I look for something to do. I need something big. Something interesting and unusual that will grab my brain so hard it will forget to think about the presents.

I wander out into the hall. I don't know what I will do next, but my feet seem to know. They start walking right toward the linen closet. I force them to take the next left, which is the bathroom. I look through a few drawers to see if there is anything interesting. I find an old-fashioned brush and use it to brush my hair to see if it will make my hair look old-fashioned, too. It doesn't. I find a pair of scissors, but put them back quick like a bunny, fast like a rabbit. Those are the things that got me in trouble last time! Then I find tweezers. I hold them up and say, "Tweezers." It is a fun word to say, so I say it again. "Tweeeeeeezers." I wonder who makes up the names of stuff like scissors and tweezers. My mom uses tweezers to pluck her eyebrows. I look at myself in the mirror, checking out my eyebrows. I wonder what my eyebrows do. Why do I have them? Why do I need them? I wonder what I would look like without them. I decide to find out.

The first pluck is the worst. After a few plucks, I teach myself a little trick. I say "pluck" every time I pluck and then I rub my eyebrow. Pluck, rub. Pluck, rub. Pluck, rub. Pretty soon it is like a little song. My fingers get tired, but I'm not a quitter and so I keep plucking until I delete one whole eyebrow.

Here is how I look with only one eyebrow: Interesting! But if I pluck out the other one, too, I will probably look like an alien, which I do not want to do. Besides, the plucking part really does hurt, even if you do the "pluck and rub" trick.

"Mary Margaret?" my mom calls from downstairs.

I smile at the new me. I have stayed away from presents and I got a new style, which is kind of like giving myself a present. "Coming, Mom," I say, giving myself a little wink. It's good to be me.

5. Uh-oh

The next morning, just when I'm fighting with my boots to get them on my feet, where they never want to go, my mom says, "Wouldn't you like to do something about that eyebrow?"

"You mean this one?" I ask, pointing to the one I still have.

"No, the other one. We could use my eyeliner pencil to draw one on. Or maybe just put on a Band-Aid."

"That would look dumb," I say.

"Which would look dumb?"

"Mo-ooom. They both would."

My mom sighs, probably because she wishes she had more style, like me. She tries a few other ideas. "How about a hat? Or a scarf? Or an eye patch, like a pirate?"

I almost say yes to the eye patch, which she pulls out of a bag and gives me. I know it would look cool on me. But I can wear an eye patch anytime. I give it back to her. "Nope. I think I'm good *oh natural*," I say. I learned that *au naturel* thing from a commercial. It means you are good the way you are.

By the time my mom and I are done having this little talk, I've missed the bus. Mom straps Liza in the car seat and drives me to school. Before I get out, she says, "I love you, Mary Margaret."

"I know," I say, unbuckling my seat belt. There are a lot of things about me to love, and because she has known me longer than just about anybody, my mom knows every single one of them. "I love you, too." Even though my mom already knows it, she still smiles like it's the first time I've ever said it.

By the time I get my boots off, I'm late. Mr. Mooney waves me over to circle time when he sees me come in the door. He is already introducing Daisy Ace's uncle. (Even though the name game is over, my brain won't stop saying middle names. I guess I trained it too well.) "I have to run down to the office for a minute," Mr. Mooney is saying to the class. "But I'm sure Mr. Winthorp will be happy to answer any and all questions you have. Keep your hands to yourself and your eyes on him, and I know we'll all learn a lot. Let's welcome him with a round of applause, shall we?"

Mr. Mooney starts us with the clapping, then leaves, but we still all clap because clapping is something we like to do. Daisy Ace claps longer than the rest of us and then adds a squeak.

Finally, Mr. Winthorp bows a little and looks around the circle at us. When his eyes land on me, he gets a funny look on his face, like he is confused. Maybe he has never seen a nine-year-old overflowing with style. At that thought, happiness fills me up and comes out my smile. After a second, he smiles back.

"Thank you," he says to all of us. "Thank you very much for inviting me today. I'd like to start by dispelling some myths. For example, the Pilgrims did not wear black-and-white clothing, except on Sunday. They wore beige, black, green, and brown. As for the Native Americans, they were probably wearing full dress, not just loincloths, since Massachusetts in November is cold. And they didn't use utensils."

To tell the truth, everything he tells us is kind of boring. I wonder when he is going to get to the good stuff—the graves and cemeteries and robbers stuff.

Jacob Xavier, who sometimes is not very good at listening, must be bored, too. He takes his eyes off Mr. Winthorp and puts them on me.

"Jeepers! What happened to you?" he whispers.

"It's my new look," I whisper back.

Ethan Liptor, who is sitting in front of us, turns around. His chin drops in shock when he sees me. "How'd you lose an eyebrow?"

"Tweeeeezers," I say.

Mr. Winthorp is done talking about utensils, I guess, because he joins our talk. "Was there a question back there?" he asks, looking right at us.

"Mary Margaret lost an eyebrow!" says Ali Jane.

After that, *nobody*'s eyes are on Mr. Winthorp anymore. Everybody's eyes are on me and the eyebrow I deleted. And then everybody's mouths start up, asking questions all at once, so I don't even know who is asking which question.

"Did you shave it?"

"Do you have cancer? Is that why your eyebrow fell out?"

"Did it hurt?"

"Will it grow back?" asks Tristan Percival.

Uh-oh. This is something I did not think of. I look at Mr. Winthorp, since he asked if we had a question back there, and now I do. "Will it grow back, Mr. Winthorp?"

And that's when I see Daisy Ace is shooting me with her eyes like I am a bad dude. Which I don't really get because all I'm doing is asking a question. Plus, Daisy Ace should be happy all the time no matter what because she has a dog, and I know that I would be happy all the time, no matter what, if I had a dog.

Right then Mr. Mooney marches in and says, "What is going on here? I could hear the noise from our room all the way down the hall."

So then Mr. Winthorp kind of explains. And then Daisy Ace gives him her idea of what happened, and it includes lots of *etceteras*. Mr. Mooney says in a voice that's stiff, "We will talk about this later." So we all know that someone is in trouble but we will have to wait to find out who. After that, we all settle down again and pretend to listen to what Mr. Winthorp has to say, even though what we are really doing is wondering who is going to be in trouble.

When Mr. Winthorp finally leaves, Mr. Mooney says he expected more of us and that we all have to stay in for recess.

"It's all your fault," says McKenzie Alice.

"I didn't start it," I say. "I didn't even ask a question until Mr. Winthorp asked if we had any."

"About the Pilgrims!" says Daisy Ace. "He wanted to know if you had questions *about the Pilgrims*, which is why he came to talk to us. He didn't come to answer questions about your stupid eyebrow and etcetera."

"Stupid?" I am suddenly getting heated up. "Well, you are—"

Ellie Paige slides up next to me and says to McKenzie Alice and Daisy Ace, "I need to borrow Mary Margaret." They harrumph away from there.

Then Ellie Paige bows her head and says very quiet, "Maybe you should go easier. You're making everybody mad."

"Mad? Daisy Ace is the one who—"

"I know," she says. "But you did kind of steal everybody's attention away from her uncle."

"Not on purpose!"

"And it's other kids, too, not just Daisy. You've been sort of wild lately, running over people's feelings. Like you don't notice anybody but you."

Ellie Paige and I are friends, but I don't get what she's saying. "I'm just being myself."

"Well, maybe, but you're acting like there are two or three of you in there," she says, poking me in the stomach, "instead of just one."

"But McKenzie Al—"

"You should probably stop using middle names. The

game is over, and we all know you won. You're just rubbing it in when you keep saying everyone's middle name."

"I'm only doing it because I trained myself to do it and now I can't untrain myself."

She puts her hand on my shoulder, which is what she does when I get overly excitable. "You could too—if you really wanted to. You can do anything if you want to bad enough."

I don't say anything back because somewhere way down deep in me, maybe even under my liver (wherever that is), I know she's right.

For the rest of the day, I untrain myself. I do it by making up a new game. After I say someone's first name, I pretend I'm out of air. I pretend if I say another word, I will melt like the Wicked Witch of the West and all that will be left of me are my clothes. Lucky for me, it works. When Daisy hands out papers, I say, "Thanks, Daisy," and I stop myself from saying "Ace." But she still scowls at me. When Noah (Bathroom Boy) comes back from the bathroom, I say, "Welcome back from the bathroom, Noah." By the end of the day, I am almost back to normal.

But at home, my mom is worse than ever. I'm doing homework at the kitchen table when my dad gets home from work, but I'm working so quietly that I can hear what they are saying in the front hall.

"I bought the hm-hm-hm today," he says. *Hm-hm-hm* must be code for "a present," but I don't know that code.

"What? You bought the hm-hm-hm? I thought we agreed to wait!"

"The thing is, I found the right one—which is hard to do, I might add—and so I made an executive decision and bought it."

"Why?"

"Because it's Christmas, Lil! You know—the season of giving?"

"Unlike Santa, we have no elves. For us to give gifts, we have to make money. And I found out today the van needs new brakes."

"Nuts!" he says. "Did you get the New Year's Eve job?"

"No, I did not," says my mom. "Which is precisely my point."

"We can afford both the hm-hm-hm and new brakes," my dad says. "You're overreacting."

"With that kind of thinking, we'll never be able to put JT through college, let alone the girls."

"We'll be fine. You're always like this when you're not making money. It's like you forget that I still am. Frankly, I'm a bit offended."

"Oh, really?" she says.

By now I am leaning so far over in my chair trying to hear every word in case they talk about the hm-hm-hm again that I almost fall off.

My dad says something I can't hear, something nice.

My mom doesn't say anything.

And that is the end of the talking, for quite a while. But

all through dinner, my parents are still saying things to each other, just without words. Mom has her arms crossed, which equals, *I'm still mad*. And Dad keeps sighing, which means, *Stop acting crazy* or maybe *Don't be such a party pooper*.

I wonder if it's bad manners to interrupt even if people aren't using words. Finally, I do. "I could eat less," I say, very helpful. "You know, so you could save money."

JT kicks me under the table. I kick him back, since it's going to be his fault if Mom and Dad save all the money for his college instead of buying more presents.

"See?" my dad says to my mom. "You're scaring the kids!"

"I'm not scared," I say. "It's just that I'd rather get presents than eat."

My mom comes around to my side of the table and bends down so she can look in my eyes. "Listen, Loverly. We have plenty of money for all the things we need, so don't worry about that."

The only thing I'm worried about is presents.

"Don't worry, Mom," says JT. "Someone will call."

She shakes her head. "I just don't understand it. I really thought the job on New Year's Eve would come through, but it hasn't yet. What's wrong with them? What's wrong with *me*?"

"Nothing!" we all say.

"You just sent those flyers," JT says. "People probably haven't gotten them yet. But when they do, they'll call."

"Thanks for the vote of confidence, JT," she says. But she's shooting my dad with her eyes while she says it.

"What?" my dad says. "I have confidence in you!"

Liza starts crying right then, because that's what she does at dinnertime. We eat. She cries. It's a pattern. But tonight I'm glad. Watching my parents zang at each other is not number one on my list of favorite things to do. And I do not want to add "Mom and Dad fight" to the dinner pattern.

A little while later, JT gets on the computer. I am minding my own beeswax until he says, "Hey, did Hannah say anything about Natalie today?"

"She wasn't at school today. What're you doing?"

"IMing with Duff—oh, wait a minute!" he says, staring at the screen. "Now Natalie is on and she wants to IM. How did she get my e-mail address?"

I shrug, very angel-like. To myself I think, Hum-de-dum, he does not sound very happy about that, so I won't tell him it might have been me, even though I am not supposed to do that. The thing is, Hannah told me I could write it *on her hand*, which made it an opportunity I couldn't pass up.

JT doesn't even have to chew on his thumbnail before he figures out it might have been me. "Stay out of my social life," he warns me.

"You mean your *love* life." Thinking about JT having a mushy gushy love life makes me laugh all the air out of me.

JT waits until I can breathe again before he says, all mad, "Just G.A., Mary Meddlesome." *G.A.* is our code for "go away."

"Hey, I was minding my own business until you dragged me into this," I say. I get my book and then flump down in the chair closest to the computer, because JT deserves to be annoyed. But he is click-click-clicking so fast on the computer that right away he forgets I'm even there. And that annoys me.

Finally, Dad asks JT to go bring the trash can in from the street and JT says, "Just a minute," three times. Then Dad says, "Now!" and JT leaves. Which works out well for me because it gives me a chance to annoy him. At first all I'm going to do is just sit in his chair and *pretend* to read what's on the screen. But that is harder than it looks, because eyes automatically read words they land on, which I did not know before. But there aren't that many words, and they aren't even real words.

> Duff: r u still in2 Nat? [Easy-peasy. It means, Are you still into Natalie?]
> JT: i guess. it's weird.
> Duff: grls r 2 hard. [Duff thinks girls are too hard.]
> JT: YGTR

Just when I'm trying to figure out what YGTR means (Your gator? Why get her?), another window pops up.

> Natalie: sorry i couldn't talk b4.

Sometimes, like now, the luck I get from my lucky pig ear stays with me for a while. I know I should tell Natalie JT is not there, just like I would on the phone, but then I would miss what she's going to say next. Which I do not want to do. So I sit very quiet like a mouse.

Natalie: now i have to go.
Me as JT:
Natalie: You must be away. CU TOM.
Me as JT:
Natalie: <3

Those little pictures you can make with punctuation marks are my very favorite thing about the computer. So when Natalie types <3, I am so eeked up that I make that little picture and send it right back to her, even though I don't know what <3 means.

Me as JT: <3
Natalie: ☺ ☺ ☺

Which means that I (as JT) made her very happy. I did a good thing.

But then I think maybe JT won't see it quite that way. There is a chance he won't like how happy "he" just made her. I x out that little chat right away so JT won't be able to see what I did when he comes back. And then I x myself right out of the room, so JT won't be able to see me, either.

6. Snow Globe, No Globe

Here's what you're going to do," says the Winter Work-shop Leader Lady, a mom who comes in every year to help us with the craft. She holds up her jar and lid above her head. "First, you take your clean jar and clean lid," she says loud and fast. "If they are not clean, go to the bathroom and wash them. No, McKenzie—not now! *After* I'm done giving the instructions. So! You take the clean lid of your clean jar and glue the knickknacks you brought—or you can use the ones we brought, there are plenty for every-one—with you to the underside of the lid. Got it? Not to the top of it. To the underside, so when you screw the lid back on, the figurines are on the inside of the jar, not on top of the jar. The PTO moms will help you because we'll be using a glue gun. That's step one. Got it? Good!

"Second, you'll put in a teaspoon of crushed eggshells. That's your snow, see? When you are done with that step, raise your hand—do not leave your seat!—just raise your hand and a PTO mom will come by and put mineral oil in. That makes the eggshells-slash-snow fall more gently than if we just used water. Got it? Good!

"Third, screw the lid of your jar tightly onto the jar. Then turn it over and—voilà! Snow globe! Any questions? No? Good! Get started. You have"—she looks at her watch—"exactly twenty-six minutes. Oh! And if you need to leave for any reason, please ask permission!"

McKenzie (I will not add *Alice*, I will not add *Alice*) shoots her hand up in the air.

"Yes, you may go wash out your jar," says the Winter Workshop Leader Lady.

I race to the table with my jar and my treasures, including the princess I broke off my music box. In the box of supplies, there are small plastic people. I find one that has brown hair like my mom. And then I find the best thing of all—a little bunny. I'm ready to start. My jar is clean. My lid is clean. I already know exactly how it will turn out—P-E-R-F-E-C-T, which spells perfect.

There is only one problem. All the things I have won't fit on my lid. I arrange them in different ways, but nothing works. I could leave something out, like the horse charm. Or the rabbit. I lay my head on the table so I can think harder. That doesn't do any good. I ask if I can go get a drink of water. The drinking fountain is down the hall, past our classroom, and around the corner. I hope that a fix to my problem will pop into my head during the long walk there and back.

It doesn't.

I sit back down in front of all the pieces of my snow globe and start a new stare-down with them.

Noah raises his hand. The Winter Workshop Leader

Lady must remember Bathroom Boy from last year, because before he even asks his question, she says, "Yes, you may go to the bathroom. Who is ready for the glue gun? Anyone?"

"I am!" says Lauren. But then she says, "Oh, wait. There's one thing I'm missing. I must have left it in my coat pocket. Can I—"

"Yes, yes, go! But no dallying. We have a schedule to keep and miles to go before we sleep!"

I'm still stuck on my snow globe problem when Lauren comes back with a little plastic Christmas tree for her globe. Hannah, who has been absent all day, is with her, and right behind her is Luke, who never even asked permission to leave.

"Sorry," Hannah says to the lady. "Dentist." Like I said, she isn't big on talking.

The Winter Workshop Leader Lady rolls her eyeballs around in her head. "Kids coming! Kids going! This place is like Grand Central Station. It'll be a miracle if any globes get made." But then she settles herself down. "Okay. Here's what you're going to do." She holds up her jar and lid above her head. "First, you take your clean jar and—oh, just ask a friend!"

Hannah thuds over to the next table, like she is weighed down and kind of stuck to the ground. It's just the way she walks. It's just the way she is. And then I look back at my trouble of a snow globe. That is when I solve my problem! Being stuck in one place is boring. The people in my snow-globe scene want to be free—not stuck to the lid. I will leave them swimming free in the snow globe, with the snow. Only instead of eggshell snow, I will use the stars and hearts for snow!

The Glue Lady comes over as soon as I raise my hand and glues the stable onto the lid. "That's it?" she asks. "You don't want anything else glued?"

"No," I say. I scoop up the two wise men, the plastic lady with brown hair, the baby Jesus in his manger, the glittery stars and hearts, the horse and dog charms, the bunny, and the rubber fish and plink them all into my big jar. Last of all, I add the princess from my music box.

The PTO lady comes over with the mineral oil. "But honey, you haven't glued them onto the lid. Did you need some help with it?"

"No, thanks," I say. "I like it this way."

"Are you sure?" she asks in a voice that means, *You're doing it wrong.*

But I'm not doing it wrong *for me.* I'm doing it just exactly right *for me.* "Yup," I say. "Just go ahead and dump that gunk in."

She looks at another PTO mom, who is actually a dad. He shrugs. "Okay, if you're sure," she says again. I guess she doesn't know how good I am at deciding things. I do not have the problem of being wishy-washy like a lot of kids.

After I screw the lid on tight, I turn it upside down and shake it. The horse and dog charms fall to the bottom with a *clunk,* but everything else floats down. A wise man gets stuck on the roof of the stable, so I jitter the jar around a little and he slides off onto the ground, next to all the others. And then the glitter stars and hearts drift down on top of everyone.

I look around at all the different kinds of snow globes kids are making. Jacob's is full of tiny soccer balls and basketballs and footballs. He's crazy about sports. Ali is concentrating so hard on gluing a tiny plane to her jar lid that if she gets any closer, her nose will end up stuck on the lid, too. She wants to fly planes when she grows up, or maybe sooner.

Their globes are cool but I like mine best. It's kind of like a Nativity scene, only with my family instead of Jesus's family. The shepherd and the wise man are like JT and my dad. The plastic lady is my mom, only a little prettier. The horse and the dog are the animals I love best, and the fish are there because they are good at floating. The baby in the manger is Liza, even if it does look like the baby Jesus. And the stable is our house.

I smile. My snow globe is just right, and my mom is going to love it.

A few minutes later the Winter Workshop Leader Lady tells us to write our names on a piece of paper and tape it to our snow globe. "Pick them up after school," she says. "We don't want any broken globes!" and she speeds us out of there, right past the next class that's waiting for their turn.

On the way back to our room, we stop at the cafeteria for juice and cookies because that is always part of Winter Workshop Day—except for Daisy, who got called down to the office, probably to get some kind of award for bringing Mr. Winthorp to our class. And etcetera.

With all that sugar and talk about presents, we are excited out by the time we stand single file outside our room, waiting for Mr. Mooney to catch up. Ellie and I are at the back of the line talking about what we would do with ten lords a-leapin' in that "Twelve Days of Christmas" song, when we hear a scream so loud it almost snaps our ears off.

"It's gone!" says Ali, who's at the front of the line.

"What's gone?" Ethan, Lauren, Jacob, Ellie, and I all ask. Caleb might have asked it, too. I'm not sure. But I know Hannah definitely was not in on the asking.

"The globe!" Ali says. "Pass it back." Pass it back, pass it up, or pass it on is the way news gets around in our class.

"The globe!" Ethan and Lauren say. "Pass it back."

"Mr. Mooney's globe!" says Jacob.

Ellie and I clap our hands to our cheeks and do a silent scream.

"Maybe Mr. Mooney took it to show someone," Ellie says.

"Maybe Mr. Mooney took it," says Jacob. "Pass it up."

"Mr. Mooney took it," says Lauren. "Pass it up."

Just then Mr. Mooney comes around the corner. "What did I take?"

"Your globe?" Ali asks with much hope in her voice.

"No, I thought I'd leave it through the holidays. You've all been so responsible and careful with it."

"Then it's missing!" Ali says. "When something is gone and no one knows where it is, it's missing!"

We all follow Mr. Mooney into our room, pushing and

bumping so we can see for ourselves what there is to see. Which is nothing. Just an empty spot where the globe used to be.

"How can this be?" asks Mr. Mooney.

"Maybe someone took it," Ali says.

"But who would do such a thing?" Mr. Mooney asks.

And even though he did not say "pass it back," suddenly it's like we are all passing that thought back. And we are all squinching up our eyes at each other. Would Ethan do it? Lauren? Hannah?

"Surely no one here would," Mr. Mooney says. "Perhaps one of the other teachers borrowed it while we were out. I'll ask around. We only have a few minutes left before the end of the day. Please just continue working on your personal webs. Don't forget to include a bit of history."

Some kids get the groans, but I like the family web. Mine is on a big sheet of paper. In the middle is a circle. In the circle is my name. Next, around that circle I am adding circles that have all the things important to me. There are circles for Mom, Dad, JT, my friend Andy, his dog Itzy, and my rabbit Hershey. It's kind of like I am the sun and all the other circles are the planets that go around me. There are also words that describe me. My words are: *naturally curious, determined, original, brave, piles of style.* I leave room to add more when I think of them. I have to add some history, so I add a circle above the circle with my mom in it and write *England and France,* because that is where my mom said our relatives were before they got started here in America. I asked my dad about his relatives.

He said they were from Neptune. He is a big kidder. Then my mom hit him, but only a fake hit, and said they were from Germany and England.

There are clumps of kids all around the class, whispering and looking all sly at the other kids. But my web is more interesting to me right now, so that's what I spend myself on.

Pretty soon McKenzie comes over. "I bet I know who did it," she says, very sure.

I pick up a red marker and draw another good circle. I like circles. They just go around and around and never end. "Really?" I ask. Because I am naturally curious. "Who?"

"You. You're the only person not whispering about who did it, and it's because you already know you did it."

That McKenzie can be so crazy. I frown, and McKenzie points at my eyebrow and laughs. And right then I know why you need eyebrows. You need them to be good at frowning, and if you only have one and try to frown, people laugh at you, which is the opposite of what they are supposed to do when you frown.

"I didn't take it," I say, because I am mostly honest, especially about big stuff. "And I'm not whispering about it because stuff at our house disappears all the time and then pops up again. I think the globe will, too."

But she isn't listening. "And I know why you did it, too," she says. "You took Mr. Mooney's because your snow globe turned out so dumb."

My insides are getting as worked up as Liza during a temper tantrum. "It's not dumb!"

"I saw it," she says. "It's just a bunch of junk floating around in the water, like trash that got dumped in the ocean."

"Don't call my family dumb," I say, huffing out the words. "Or my snow globe, which is a Nativity scene of my family."

"That's what I mean. A Nativity scene of your family. How dumb is that? Plus, they all float all around!"

"I wanted it that way," I say. "They are floating around because I didn't think JT or my mom or dad would want to be stuck to one spot. And when you shake us up, we all end up back at home."

McKenzie has a "yeah, right!" look on her face, which makes me add, "And I haven't even done the best part yet! The best part is I'm going to put a light underneath it, so my mom can use it as a night-light in her room."

"You can say what you want," she says. "But I know the truth." And then she flounces back to her desk.

"Yeah, well, the truth is, my snow globe is a marvel," I yell after her. "You're just jealous because it's not boring, like yours." I didn't actually see McKenzie's snow globe, but I'm pretty sure it must be boring.

When Mr. Mooney comes back, he doesn't have good news. "It appears that the snow globe is indeed missing," he says. "I hate to think someone here in our troupe took it, but . . . let's do this. It has been a long day. And it's still possible that another teacher borrowed it. So let's just leave this lie until tomorrow morning. With any luck, it will turn up by then. Let's hustle into our coats so we have time to retrieve our snow globes and still catch our buses home."

In the hall, we pull on our coats and hats. I skip my boots because I want to be speedy quick to get to my beautiful snow globe. It might not look anything like Mr. Mooney's globe, but it is like Mr. Mooney's in one way. It's a rare find and one of a kind.

My mom is not home when I get there, only JT, who is in his room.

I am so excited to show him what I made that I burst right through his door.

"Where's Mom?" I ask.

"Obviously you're flunking that Knocking 101 class you signed up for," he says without even looking up from his book.

"Oh, sorry. Where is she?"

"Liza. Doctor."

"Want to see the present I made her?" I am already pulling it out of my backpack.

"Not really."

This cuts into my heart. "But . . . why not?"

"Maybe because I'm in the middle of something else. Or could be because I'm annoyed by how you just barge in here and I'm not in the mood to admire whatever little doodad you made for Mom at the moment." It's a mean thing to say, especially for JT, who is usually a brother plus a friend.

"It's not a doodad. It's a work of art."

His eyes stay on his book, but his hand waves at me. "Bye-bye, Mary Masterpiece," he says.

I slam his door and stomp away. He'll be sorry. I'll wrap the present right now and he won't get a chance to see it until Christmas morning.

To make the present extra special, I make the wrapping paper, too. I get out a big roll of butcher paper that my mom keeps around for me because I am so creative. Then I get to work drawing. I draw me and my mom in swimsuits. I make my swimsuit lime green and purple and very sassy. I make her swim suit dark blue, and give it a turtleneck. I draw me and my mom at the zoo. I put me next to a wallaby, lemur, and koala bear. I put her next to a sheep, and make it very fluffy and tame. I draw an airplane and show me jumping out of it with a parachute. I leave my mom in the plane because I'm pretty sure that is where she would want to be.

I'm ready to wrap the present when I remember I can't yet because I want to add a light on the bottom of the snow globe. For that I need JT, who isn't my favorite person right now. So I have to wait. Then things get dangerous because those pesky presents my mom hid in her bedroom start calling to me.

"Mary Margaret, come find us!" they whisper. I don't listen.

The presents giggle like it's a game. "Don't you want to know what we are?"

I wish I already had the pair of handcuffs I asked for, because I would handcuff my hand to the stair rail to keep myself from peeking at those presents. "Not until Christmas," I say.

"We could make you happy! We could make you happy right now!"

Hmmm, I think. I could use a happiness right now. Plus, the presents would make me happy now *and* on Christmas. That is like a double good deal. Four big tiger leaps and I would be there. Maybe even three, if they were supersized. I crouch into leaping position, ready to go to the presents, when the doorbell rings.

I bound down the stairs because bounding is what tigers do and look out the peephole. There are two girls standing there. One is holding a little heart pillow. I open the door but just enough to stick my lips out. They don't look dangerous, but you never know. "Yes?" I say.

There is some giggling, then one of them says, "Is JT home?"

"Just a minute," I say. I shut the door and then turn and roar up the stairs, louder than I have to, "JT, TWO GIRLS ARE HERE FOR YOU!"

Then I sit on the bottom step and wait because I think this might be interesting. Too bad I didn't know what they would say, and then what JT would say back. If I had known all that, I would have bounded right out of the house and out of the United States of America.

"Hey, Taylor. Hi, Natalie," JT says. "Come on in."

So they do, and then they all stand around in the front hall, not really looking at each other. Which is why I finally say, "I'm Mary Margaret."

"Oh, yeah," says Natalie. "Mary Margaret Mary." But she says it like she's serious, not like she's teasing. So I guess JT didn't tell her that I don't really have a middle name. Which is a big relief because I wouldn't want that news to get around.

It seems like no one else is going to say anything again, which doesn't seem very productive. So I say, "Nice pillow."

Natalie smiles. "Thanks."

Taylor elbows her, but Natalie shakes her head. Taylor rolls her eyeballs and takes the pillow and holds it out to JT. "It's for you," she says. "Squeeze it."

JT's cheeks turn red. "Oh, um, okay."

Then the pillow says, "Hi, JT," only in Natalie's voice.

JT turns even redder. "Um, thanks, I guess," he says, but he looks like he doesn't really get it. Taylor must think so, too, because she elbows Natalie again. But Natalie shakes her head even harder and whispers, "No, you."

"After last night, she wanted to give you a real heart. Well, not real-real, but more real than an emoticon."

"Last night?" JT says.

"Yeah, when you were IMing, and Natalie sent you a heart?"

Uh-oh. So that's what <3 means. It's a heart.

Taylor is still talking. "And then after a few minutes you sent her one back. It was around seven-thirty; right, Nat?"

JT suddenly gets it and shoots me a dirty look. "Oh, yeah, that. Um, well, thanks!"

"Well, that's all we stopped by for, so I guess we'll go," says Taylor.

Natalie smiles and says, "Bye, Mary Margaret Mary."

"Oh! I should have told you the other day. Mary Margaret doesn't have a middle name," JT says. And he smiles at me very sweet. "It's just Mary Margaret."

"Oh!" says Natalie. "In that case, bye, Just Mary Margaret."

JT laughs. "Good one," he says.

As Taylor and Natalie leave, I turn to scamper out of there, because I don't much feel like a tiger anymore, but more like a chipmunk and I want to run for my burrow, but JT grabs me by the collar and shakes the heart pillow at me. "It was you, wasn't it? You answered her heart with a heart and she thought it was me."

"I was just being polite," I say. "I didn't know it was a heart! It looked more like a math to me."

"You made everything worse!"

"But you got a pillow."

"You don't get it. Now we're going together *with hearts*! I don't want hearts."

"Why didn't you just tell her that, then?"

"This isn't about me. It's about how you never think how what you do might affect someone else."

"Me? What about what *you* did?" I say. "You promised you wouldn't tell about the name game and then you did and you know what? It's going to make troubles for me at school."

"Welcome to my world," he says. "You've been making troubles for me since the day you were born."

That's not a very nice thing to say, even if it's true.

7. Booted

Going to school the next morning is not my favorite thing to do. Because by now Natalie has probably told Hannah that I don't really have a middle name, and Hannah will blab about it at school. Everybody will be mad, even though all I did was stretch the truth a little bit, like my mom did when she said she mopped the floor in the laundry room because she didn't want us in there. It's not fair that grown-ups can stretch the truth all over the place but I can't. But I know that grown-ups don't use the same rules they make kids use.

I almost miss the bus because I, very grumpy, am looking all over for my boots. Finally, I remember I left them at school.

"Looks like you're starting your day off on the wrong foot," my dad says.

"Ha-ha," I say, but I have a feeling this is not going to be a laughing kind of day.

I'm right about that in a few ways. For example, the missing globe that is still missing.

"I sent an e-mail to all the teachers and even our janitor, Mrs. Capotosto," says Mr. Mooney. "Let's see what the day brings."

The day does not bring Hannah, who is absent. Lucky for me.

But it does bring math and recess, where nothing interesting happens, and gym class, where we learn to dance the Macarena. It's a good day until after lunch, when we are settling down to desk work.

Because that is when Hannah arrives. She clods over to my desk and grins down at me. "I know," she says.

"Know what?"

"I know you know what I know," she says. "But I'll say it *out loud* if you really want me to."

"That's okay," I say.

"I won't tell anyone, though."

This is a shocker. "You won't?"

"Not if you tell me what JT likes so Natalie can buy him a present."

"She already bought him a heart pillow!" I say, wondering why he gets presents even though he doesn't want them. Those presents just go to waste on him.

"She wants to get him a *Christmas* present," Hannah says. "Something he'll really *like*. Because she really *likes* him."

"Yeah," I say. "I get that. Um, he likes stuff for his computer—and music! He likes music. And he likes to run." In my head, I add, *Away from your sister,* but I don't say that out loud because she probably would not think it was funny.

Hannah puts her hands on either side of my book and leans very close to me. "So she could get him . . . what?" Her breath smells like old cherry Life Savers.

"Well, I got him Tetranamous, a computer game that he thinks looks cool."

"We'll take it!" she says.

"You mean you want the present I bought for JT? So Natalie can give it to him?"

She steps back from my desk and smiles. "Yeah. Natalie will pay you for it."

"But that was my best idea for him. You can't just take it. It's not fair."

"Neither is the way you won the name game."

I flap my mouth open and closed two times, but no words come out.

When Hannah sees that I don't have anything to say, she says, "Don't worry. Your secret is safe with me," and walks away.

Things get a little better when the day brings chocolate cupcakes because it's Noah's birthday.

But what the day never ever brings is the globe.

Mr. Mooney asks us to put our work away early and says, "It's very upsetting to me to think that someone among us has taken it, but everyone has lapses in judgment. So I'm going to grant clemency, amnesty, and anonymity to the culprit. After all, it is Chri—*the holidays,* a time of generosity of spirit. Therefore, I'm going to let the person who took the globe go without consequences, if he or she will return it," he says. "We'll go to the cafeteria and then each of you will walk by yourself to the bathroom. If there is nothing on your conscience"—Mr. Mooney stares hard at us—"and you know what I mean, then you will just come back to the cafeteria. But for the person who has something to do—that is, put the globe in my closet—you will do the right thing and then come back to the cafeteria with a clear conscience and no one else ever has to know."

So that's why we end our day sitting in the cafeteria and watching each other leave for and come back from the bathroom. Bathroom Boy/Noah sighs with happiness. But the rest of us sag and slump in our seats, waiting for our turn.

When it's my turn, I walk to the bathroom. I look at my eyebrow in the mirror, and it looks good. Then I try to frown and it does look a little silly. I hope my eyebrow grows back quickly so I can frown like I mean it.

When every person has taken their turn, we make our way back to the classroom.

Too bad the globe doesn't.

As we all find our seats, Mr. Mooney lifts his glasses up and rubs his eyes. "Ladies and gentlemen, we have reached a disappointing end to our otherwise lovely day. I think we all need to go home, get a good night of sleep, and revisit this in the morning. To the hall, good fellows, for your cloaks and wraps and boots." Mr. Mooney always talks this way. It's a little strange, but we're used to it.

Mr. Mooney asks us to be quiet in the hall and "think about the importance of honesty," but I am too busy fighting with my boots to think about anything. My boots have a mind of their own and do not cooperate. I get my left boot on, finally, but when I stick my other foot in my other boot, it gets only halfway in before it bumps into something.

"Hurry up, Mary Margaret!" says Caleb.

"I'm trying," I say, very frustrated. "But something is stuck in there." I yank my foot out and then reach down with my hand to pull out . . . *uh-oh!* My fingers know what it is before my brain does. If my brain knew, it would tell my arm to STOP RIGHT THERE, MISSY! But my arm is already pulling and it keeps pulling until everyone can see what my fingers already know.

The thing stuck in my boot is Mr. Mooney's globe.

Everyone gasps. My mouth drops open. I feel funny inside, like my guts are turning into a hunk of ice. I hold the globe out in front of me. But how—? Who—? Why—? Question words swirl around in my head, but I can't make them line up into a real question. I stand there, swaying in front of the globe. I can't drag my eyes off it, but I'm not really seeing it, either. When I finally make my eyes focus, I see everyone standing there all puffed up in their coats and hats and boots, staring at me not moving. And I know what they are thinking. *Globe + Mary Margaret's boot = Mary Margaret did it. Mary Margaret stole the globe.*

Then the rest of me turns into ice, too.

8. I Am Not a Robber!

I knew it," says McKenzie, crossing her arms, very dramatic.

I look down at the globe, then up again. Ellie's face is all wrinkled, like she's going to cry. Kyle, Jacob, Caleb, and Tristan look at me like I have changed into a monster with orange scales and a pointed tail that shoots fire. Lauren and Ali just stare down at their boots, like they can't stand to look at me. Arial is grinning like she thinks it's all big fun. Daisy doesn't look surprised at all.

"I didn't do it," I say. "I don't know how it got there, but I didn't take it. Honest!"

Hannah smirks. "You mean honest like 'My name is Mary Margaret *Mary*' honest?"

Uh-oh, I think.

Now everyone is looking at her. "She doesn't have a middle name," she says. "My sister is going out with her brother and he says she doesn't have a middle name."

"Hannah!" I say. "You promised."

She shrugs. "Changed my mind."

Mr. Mooney shakes his head slowly, which means I'm

a big disappointment to him. He reaches out for the globe. "Mary Margaret, you stay. Everyone else is dismissed."

When everyone is gone, he says, "Put your other boot on, Mary Margaret, and follow me."

I do not want to follow Mr. Mooney. I would rather wear boring clothes for the rest of my life than follow Mr. Mooney. I would rather spend twenty-four or more hours a day with my screaming baby sister than follow Mr. Mooney. But it doesn't seem like that is a choice of mine, so I follow.

He perches on the edge of his desk and looks at me.

"I didn't do it!" I blurt out. "I'm telling the truth!"

"The name game?"

I hang my head. "I did do that."

"Mary Margaret, you are a joy to have in the classroom. You are curious and intelligent. But why must you always push? And this time you went beyond pushing! Why lie?"

"I just wanted to play the game."

"And win."

"But I didn't steal the globe! This time I'm telling the truth. The true one hundred percent truth."

"I want to believe you, I really do," he says. "But your actions show what you are made of. Once people see you as a liar, it's hard for them to believe anything you say. Besides, it was in your boot. I'm afraid I will have to call your parents."

My icy insides crack up into chips right then and push themselves right up into my eyes, where they melt into tears. "Please, please don't!" Then I boo-hoo out,

"It's-not-fair-It-wasn't-me-Just-give-me-a-chance-please-just-a-chance-before-you-call-because-if-you-don't-I'll-never-get-to-see-the-World-Famous-Lip-Lip-Lipizzaner-Stallions-Show!"

And then I think of the worst thing of all. *Santa!* Somehow, now that Mr. Mooney knows that I made a bad choice about the name game, Santa will, too. And that makes me cry even harder.

"Mary Margaret, calm down and take a breath."

I suck in a giant gulp of air and drop onto my knees. "Please! I'm begging you! My parents mean it when they say I won't be able to go. And my mom is already in a bad mood because her clients aren't calling. And there are unwrapped presents hidden in our house and I know where all of them are and that's a tragedy and this will make it all worse. Please give me a chance."

Mr. Mooney hands me a Kleenex. I mop up my eyes and my nose, which has also been leaking. I also stand up because my bony knees are starting to hurt.

"Okay, I don't really understand about you and the Lipizzaners," he says.

"The World Famous Lipizzaner Stallions Show," I say with a sniffle. Because you have to be respectful of those beasts.

Mr. Mooney ignores that and says, "But I don't need to. What I understand is that you want a chance, and I'm willing to give it to you."

"Because it's Christmas?" I say.

"That's part of the reason, but mostly it's because I want

to believe in you again. I hope you didn't do it. Frankly, I hope none of my students did it. I'll give you one day—two, tops—before I call your parents."

"Thank you! Thank you from the bottom of my heart."

I run like a gust to catch my bus. Once I'm on, I scuffle up the aisle, past whispers and past staring faces, to a seat that's empty. Because no one wants to sit with a thief, or even someone they think is a thief. I keep my chin up, though, because I know something they don't. I know they are wrong about me.

At home I rip my list of presents off the refrigerator. All I want right now is for people to know the truth. I might have told a little white lie about my name, but I did not steal the globe. I am not a robber! I wad up my list and throw it in the garbage. I don't want a talking monkey (NOT REAL) or a Clever Heifer. I don't care about plastic handcuffs, a puppy, the Breyer horse and barn set, or any of the other stuff on my stupid wish list.

Then I put myself on pause. Because my list isn't completely stupid. And I do care a little bit about the plastic handcuffs, because they would be useful for playing with Jolene, and someday Liza, probably. And I care about the dog. Because having a dog is a lifelong dream of mine.

I pluck my list out of the garbage, but only the first page, which has the sixteen things I want the most. I smooth it out over my leg before I put it back where it belongs—right on the fridge, where my mom can see it. And Santa, too. Because he might see things the same way as me, which is that I maybe made one bad choice, but I've been nice a lot more than I've been naughty.

I slump around so much that my mom finally asks me what's wrong.

"Just tired," I say. I start reading a book that's so good it makes me and my life invisible and I'm in a whole different world—until JT barges in, grabs my hand, and pulls me out of that world.

"Come on," he says. "You're going shopping with me. Mom said she'd drop us at the mall for a little while."

I yank my hand away. "No, I'm not. I hate shopping and I hate the mall. Besides, I'm booked," I say, waving my book in front of his face, very pleased with myself.

JT doesn't laugh or even smile. "Look, you got me into this. The whole girl thing is . . ." He flings his hands up. "*Pi-kew!* Like an explosion. Out of control. Everyone thinks Natalie and I are boyfriend and girlfriend instead of just going together. It's your fault. You *owe* me. And this is how you're going to pay up—by helping me find a present for Natalie."

The whole time he's talking, I'm all ready to dig in my feet and say I'm not going. Then he gets to the word *present*, and that reminds me about all the presents in the house and about my new rule, which is never ever let myself be alone in the house. Because those things are not resistible.

The mall is like one huge birthday party. Everybody is carrying bags of presents and it's loud and it seems like everyone has had too much cake and other sugar because even the grown-ups are all stirred up. My mom says she's taking Liza and going for a cup of coffee and she'll meet us in an hour.

"A whole hour?" I ask. "Why do we need all that time to find a present for a g—"

"Okay, Mom!" JT says, putting his arm around my shoulder and rushing me away from there. When we're down the hall, he says, "I told you not to say anything in front of her."

"All right, all right!" I say, feeling cranky because I'm bumping into so many people and packages that I feel like a bumper car. "Can we just get this over with?" But then I think, Maybe shopping with JT will give me a new idea about what to buy him, since Hannah stole my old idea.

I pick up a pair of fluffy pink mittens. "These are nice. How about these?"

"I don't know. She isn't really a fluffy kind of girl."

"What kind of girl is she?"

"I don't know," he says, all annoyed. "Just keep looking, Mary Merchandise."

I do, because at least that way I don't have to think about my troubles.

I stroke soft stuffed animals, but JT says stuffed animals are too cutesy. I sniff smelly perfume, but JT says perfume is too romantic. I try on a necklace, but JT says necklaces are too serious. I hold up a bracelet, but JT says bracelets are too serious. I line up rings on all my fingers, but JT says rings are too serious. And when I say, "Then how about earrings?" he snaps, "All jewelry is too serious! No jewelry!"

"Why didn't you just say that to begin with?" I say. "And if you don't even like her, why can't you just buy her any old thing?"

"Because I like her, I just don't *like* her like her."

"So?"

"So, now Natalie thinks we're boyfriend/girlfriend, and now that it's gone that far, I'm going to have to break up with her!"

"Then why are you being so picky about her present?"

"*Because* I'm going to break up with her!" he says in a loud voice he doesn't use that often.

I just stare at him. I still don't get it.

He sighs and leans against the counter. "I feel bad about breaking up with her, so I want to get her something she'll like, KWIM?"

"Sort of," I say.

"I guess that's good enough," he says. He lets out a sigh like he has big troubles. "Think, Mary Margaret. Is there anything Hannah said that could help me pick something Natalie would like? I could use your help here."

My heart melts all down the sides of my insides right then. JT needs me. Before, all this shopping felt like a chore. But now that JT needs me, it feels more like we are playing a game—and we're even on the same team.

I close my eyes and think hard. And then I do remember something.

"She likes polka dots," I say. "But not just ordinary polka

dots. New polka dots, which I don't even know about."

JT grins. "I do!" he says. "It's a band. She likes the New Polka Dots." And then he does something he never does. He hugs me right there in front of everybody. Like he doesn't even mind that I'm his little sister.

After we buy the CD and are walking back to meet Mom, he says, "You were a big help figuring out that problem. Thanks!"

"If only I could figure out mine," I mutter.

"What?" he says.

"Nothing," I say. Because if I tell JT, there's a chance he'll tell Mom and Dad, like he told Natalie about the name game.

"Come on," he says. "Maybe I can help. As long as it doesn't involve thirteen-year-old girls, I'm pretty good at stuff. You know I'm smart—come on, admit it."

"Smarter than a bird, maybe," I say. JT really is smart, but I would never tell him.

"Does that mean I'm not a birdbrain?"

That makes me smile, even though I am not in a smiling mood.

"We still have a few minutes. I'll buy you a cookie and you can tell me all about it."

"I'll take the cookie, but I don't want to talk about it."

"All right," he says, like he doesn't care.

"Okay," I say, like I don't care that he doesn't care.

But then while I'm eating my cookie, he asks me about school, and I tell him about the snow globes we made on Winter Workshop Day, and then I tell him about how Mr.

Mooney had a really cool globe. By then, my mouth is all warmed up from all that talking and it just keeps going until it tells him that the globe was missing but now it's not anymore because it turned up. In my boot.

"What? Did you take it?"

"No, but everyone thinks I did. Why do they?"

"It's pretty hard to ignore that it was in your boot. Also, you have a way of seeing things differently than everyone else."

"But that's a good thing. I'm unique."

"You can be unique without thinking the world is all about you."

"I don't think that!"

"Hmmm," he says. "What are you getting Mom for Christmas?"

"You know what I'm getting her because you helped me order it! It's a mug."

"With a picture of who on it?"

"Me."

"And what are you getting Dad?"

"You know that, too! A cap."

"With a . . . ?"

"Picture of me on it."

"And for Liza?"

"A bib!" which JT also knows. It has a picture of me on it, too.

"I don't know what you're getting me, but I'm guessing it's a T-shirt with a picture of you on it."

"Well, you're wrong." I would have gotten him that,

though, if I hadn't needed his help ordering it. "What's wrong with those presents?"

"There's nothing wrong with them. I'm just saying you think everything exists for you. So I guess I could see you thinking that about things, too. Like even if they aren't exactly yours, they kind of are. Maybe you'd see something that way."

But I don't hear anything he says because I am thinking about how good I did on presents, especially the game I bought for him but now won't be able to give to him. "Mom says to pick something you think the other person will like, not that you like. Mom will like a mug because she likes coffee. Dad always wears caps. And Liza likes to spit up."

JT throws up his hands. "See? You completely miss that maybe they don't want pictures of *you* on their presents."

JT is not helping me here. All he is doing is taking us off the subject. "I *didn't* take the globe," I grumble.

"Okay, you didn't take it. Maybe you were framed. Someone set you up and made it look like you did it."

"Mr. Mooney is going to call Mom and Dad unless I can prove I didn't do it. And then they won't let me go to the World—"

"Famous Lipizzaner Stallions Show," JT says. He thinks he is so smart. "When you're thinking about who did it, remember two words—*motive* and *opportunity*. Who would've wanted it to look like you took the globe and who had the chance to steal it."

"I have a different recipe," I say.

"That figures. What is it?"

"This plus this," I say, patting my head and then my gut. "My brain will get me started and then I will get a gut feeling. That's my recipe. But I think what you said is good, too, in its own way."

"I'd wish you luck, but I have a feeling a few other kids in the class need it worse than you."

He's right. Because whoever really did take the globe apparently does not know something. He or she picked the wrong person to set up and frame.

9. Scrooge, Pollyanna, and a Janitor

As long as Loudmouth Liza isn't around, the kitchen table is a good place for thinking. That's because it's close to snacks, and I can't think if my brain is hungry. So that is where I settle down to do some desk work before bed. I get some crackers and cheese and start making a list.

Lists are very productive things. They can help you remember to buy things (like presents), feed things (like Hershey), and find crooks and cheats, like I'm not sure who yet but I am working on it.

Who stole Mr. Mooney's globe and put it in my boot
1. <u>Not ME!</u> (never, ever in a katrillion years)
2. Hannah (changes her mind in a snap) (and also scary)
3. Arial/Whopper Girl (very good at lying)
4. McKenzie (never sees I to I with me, due to I am always right and she is always wrong)

I told JT that my brain + my guts will tell me who did it. I let my brain work on it for a while.

The snow globe wasn't missing when we left for the Winter Workshop. It was missing when we got back. So somebody must have taken it while we were making our globes. I remember the Winter Workshop Lady called it Grand Central Station because kids kept pulling in and out of there, so lots of somebodies could have done it.

Me, because I left to get a drink. Except I know for real and for true that it's not me.

Noah/Bathroom Boy, because he went to the bathroom.

And lots of other people who I can't remember right now.

Scratch! goes my pencil right through Hannah's name. She didn't even come until late that day. Or . . . was that the day we talked about JT's present?

And then I get a little off subject with myself because I start thinking about the Christmas presents I'll be getting, once I fix my whole big trouble. Santa might even get me extra presents because he'll feel bad about having me on the naughty list, where I don't belong.

Thinking about presents puts me very in the Christmas spirit, so I go to the coat closet and scrummage around on the floor, which is where all the leftovers of mittens and hats are, until I find my Santa hat from last year. It's a red hat with a rim of green fur and a green ball on the end, because red and green are Santa's team colors, which everyone knows.

After admiring myself in the front-hall mirror, I wander back to the kitchen because I want to finish my list, but, too bad for me, the laundry-room door is open a crack. Which is loud enough to hear the hm-hm-hm present giggling. I guess I have been exercising my self-control muscle so hard that it is worn out, because suddenly I am in that laundry room zipping through cupboards like somebody pushed my fast-forward button. What is the hm-hm-hm? Is it for JT or for me? If Mom was mad about Dad buying it, then it must have cost a lot. And if it cost a lot, it must be something really big and exciting.

The weird thing is that every time I open a cupboard door, I kind of hope the hm-hm-hm is not there, because there's the slice of me (good) that doesn't want to know what I'm getting for Christmas. But when it's not there, I can't stop myself from looking in the next cupboard because of the other slice of me (bad) that wants to know. Mom and Dad are upstairs giving Liza a bath, and JT is in his room, so I probably won't get discovered snooping. But I kind of wish someone would discover me before I discover the hm-hm-hm. Except that I don't want to get in trouble.

But no one comes. Instead, the way it goes is, I fling a cupboard open, paw through it, then fling the door closed, all as fast as I can. It's not in the mop closet. Or in the detergent cupboard. I check behind the ironing board. Nothing! I look everywhere—even in the washer and dryer. No hm-hm-hm.

I am disappointed but also relieved. I guess that

means I'm disapprelieved. I slink out of there—right into my dad.

"Looking for something?" he asks.

"Ummm, yeah, I was looking for my Santa hat," I say, which is a true thing. Because I *was* looking for my Santa hat. A while ago.

"Ha! It's right here on your head!" he says, patting it.

"I know," I say, bending my lips into a smile. "I found it. Isn't that great? I'm so happy I found it because it puts me in the Christmas spirit, where I definitely want to be. Right there. In the Christmas spirit!" I'm talking very fast, which is what I do when I'm nervous. "Now I can go back to making my list of . . . um . . . people I like. I have a lot of people to add to that list! Daisy, Ellie, Noah, Tristan, Mr. Mooney, Hershey. It's going to be a long list, so I have to get busy on it!"

"Will it be as long as your Christmas list?"

"Oh, no. I made that thing shorter."

"Oho! I doubt that," he says. "That would be the Eighth Wonder of the World."

That hurts my feelings a little bit. I frown, which makes my dad laugh. And that makes me remember about my missing eyebrow and how no one takes me seriously when I only have one eyebrow. I try a foot stamp. "I really did! It was too full, so I emptied a few things off it so you wouldn't have so much to remember."

"In that case, thank you. That was very considerate of you."

"You're welcome," I say. Then I beat it out of there

before he can change the subject back to the laundry room, where I was not supposed to be.

Once I'm back in my room, I remember that I forgot my list of maybe-thieves. If my dad sees it, he will ask me hard questions I don't want to answer until I have better answers that will explain everything. The answers I have right now would mean no World Famous Lipizzaner Stallions Show for me.

On my way back downstairs, I hear my dad say, "Where, exactly, did you put the hm-hm-hm, Lil? I can't wrap it if I can't find it."

I stop and perk my ears up.

"The hm-hm-hm? Oh, I made an executive decision and took that back."

"What? Do you know how hard those are to find?"

"Very, apparently," says my mom in her "oh, well" voice.

"Yes, very," says my dad in his "I'm not very happy" voice. "That gift would have made the kids' Christmas!"

"They'll survive. We can't afford it right now."

"Scrooge," my dad says.

"Pollyanna!"

My parents are calling each other names, which we are not supposed to do. Ever. Hearing them shoot names at each other jangles me all up, because it's their job to get along. And if they are not doing that job, then maybe they'll stop doing the other things parents are supposed to do.

I'm ready to jump in and tell them to stop it, but just

then the back door slams and I hear JT say, "Man, it's cold out there! What's going on?"

"Nothing!" say my mom and dad at the same time, both very bright. Which would be an example of them stretching the truth.

JT doesn't know that things aren't right here. "Is there anything good to eat?" he asks.

Very relieved that he stopped the fight, I grab my list and go to my room. But I can't stop thinking about the missing globe. Or about how my parents are arguing. Suddenly I'm exhausted, which used to be my mom's favorite word. (And which I like because the word sounds the same way you feel, like all the air is pushed out of you. Ex-*auuuuuus*-ted.) I hop into bed and pull up the covers.

Even though the rest of me is lying very still, my brain is still running laps inside my head. I give it the job of making up new verses for my "Jingle Bells" song. I keep the chorus the same, though. The reasons I should get what I want are still good, even if what I want has changed.

This is what I want
For Christmastime this year
I know I've changed my mind
But, Santa, listen here!
I want people to know
I sometimes do stuff wrong
But I would never steal
I know where things belong!

Oh, I've set the table
When I was able
Been nice to Jolene
Cheered JT
Cleaned up pee
Nev-er acted me-ean.
I make my bed
See Hershey's fed
Make sure I'm not bored
I never curse, I could be worse
And that's worth a reward!

And then there's Mom and Dad
Not acting like themselves
You need to make them stop
And hear those Christmas bells
I don't need peace on earth
That's way too much to ask
Just some peace at home
Please get to that one fast!

If you have the time,
I like a good surprise-ah
Some presents would be nice
(But not one like Eliza!)

But before I can make up a verse with all the presents I still want, my brain falls off the edge right into sleep.

———

I guess my gut does work even when my brain and the rest of me is asleep, because as soon as I wake up the next morning, my gut tells me who took the globe. That's a big relief. Now I can prove it in front of all the kids and Mr. Mooney and Santa. And then the thief will be sorry she tried to make me look evil.

Too bad it doesn't work out quite that way.

At school, I wait until Mr. Mooney has told us the announcements for the day and asked if anyone had any announcements *related to our day*. He always adds that part, otherwise some kids (not me, except sometimes) will talk about what they learned about dogs or about the football game that was on last night. So he always says "related to our day." Which my announcement definitely is.

I raise my hand. "I didn't take your snow globe. McKenzie did."

Everybody gasps. "Yup," I say. "McKenzie is Robber Girl."

"No, I'm not!" McKenzie says. She is a very good actor, because she says it like she really isn't the robber, when I know for a fact that she is. "That doesn't even make any sense. Why would I take it? I *like* my own snow globe. My snow globe turned out perfect, not like yours with everything bobbing around in the water all over the place and—"

Mr. Mooney holds up his hand to make McKenzie stop yapping.

"This is very serious," he says to me. "Are you sure you're not jumping to conclusions?"

"Yes, I'm sure. It was McKenzie and I can tell you proof

of it." And then everyone starts chattering like teeth do when you get really cold. Mr. Mooney has to put up his hand again and say, "Class, class!" until everyone quiets down.

"Let's listen to why Mary Margaret thinks it's McKenzie. It could be very instructive." Mr. Mooney likes things that are instructive, and I'm thinking this is a good sign for me. "As long as it's all right with you, McKenzie."

"Okay," says McKenzie. "But I get a turn to talk, too."

"Of course," says Mr. Mooney. "Mary Margaret, you may begin."

"I have three good reasons," I say. "My first one is that she left the Winter Workshop to wash out her jar, which she was supposed to have done before she even got there. So she had the chance to take the globe. Second, before we knew for sure the globe was really missing, McKenzie told me she knew I did it. And the reason she 'knew' I did it was because she had already put the globe in my boot." I smile, very happy with how smart I am.

"And the third reason?" Mr. Mooney asks.

"Oh. Hmmm," I say, because I have forgot the third reason. But then I remember it again. "She doesn't like me on account of I'm right and she isn't. Oh—and another proof is she is a sore loser at me because I won the name game." But then I wish my mouth had slowed down because I remember that everyone knows I didn't actually win that game fair and square.

"All right. McKenzie? Your rebuttal?"

Jacob, Caleb, Ethan, and Tristan get all snickery when Mr. Mooney says "rebuttal" because it has the word *butt* in it.

McKenzie says, "I did not steal the globe and I can *prove* it, if you let me go get Mrs. Capotosto." So she does.

It only takes a minute. "Mrs. Capotosto," says McKenzie, all formal, when they get back. Inside myself I groan, because I can see she is pretending to be a lawyer, which is what her dad is. "Remember on Winter Workshop Day when I almost knocked you down coming out of the workshop room?"

"I do," says Mrs. Capotosto. "You apologized and said you needed to wash out your jar."

"Then what happened?"

"I said I'd better come down and help you because that faucet has been acting up, and if you turn the water on too high, it'll spout out all over the room. And that's one mess I didn't want to have to clean up again. I've done it enough times with all the teachers making that mistake!"

Everybody laughs because it's funny to think about teachers getting sprayed all over.

"And did you leave after I washed out my jar?"

"Let me think," she says. "No, no. I remember the office paging me right then to tell me the heat in the library wasn't working very well, so I had to walk back down past the workshop room anyway, so you and I walked together."

"Would you say, then, that we were together the entire time I was not in the Winter Workshop?"

"Yes."

"And did you ever see me take a snow globe from this room?"

"You weren't even ever in this room, sweetheart."

"I rest my case," says McKenzie, putting her nose in the air like she's so smart.

"Thank you, Mrs. Capotosto," says Mr. Mooney. "I hope this shows that we can't have people just running willy-nilly all over the school falsely accusing others of serious crimes."

And even though that is exactly what happened to me, I don't get the chance to say so. Because Mr. Mooney says, "Moving right along!" And moves us right into math. Besides, I'm pretty sure nobody would believe me right then, anyway.

10. Gotcha!

There are a million kids it could have been," Ellie says at lunch recess. "Why did you think it was McKenzie?"

"I had a gut feeling," I say, a little glum. Because since I said it was McKenzie and she proved it wasn't, everybody is twice as sure that it was me. And they aren't being very nice about it. At lunch, Kyle kept holding up his fork and looking at me through it, so it looked to him like I was behind bars in jail. "You're in jail!" He giggled. Then everyone started doing it. The worst part is that, with all of them staring at me through their forks teasing me, I really did feel like I was in jail. I pulled my legs up to my chest and wrapped my arms around them, because I wanted to fold myself up into a shell so their words would just bounce off me. But my words bounce off them instead. The more I say I didn't do it, the more positive they are that I did.

And even before that happened, Mr. Mooney said he didn't like the way this was going, and if I didn't know anything new by the end of the day, he was going to call my parents. If only I had my lucky pig ear, all this would probably go a lot better for me.

"Plus, she was mad at me." I say. "I thought that was good enough."

"I want to help you," Ellie says, "but first promise you won't get mad at me."

"Why would I get mad at you for trying to help me?"

"Because you won't like what I'm going to say. Promise you won't get mad?"

"I promise," I say, because I don't think she can say anything that will make me feel any worse than I already feel.

"You've been kind of pushy and, well, rude lately—just a little," she says very fast.

"I'm being myself," I say.

"Remember when I said it seemed like there were two of you inside your skin instead of just one?"

I nod.

Ellie nods back. "So . . . yeah, it's been like that."

"Well, even if it has been like that, what does it have to do with the globe?"

"If we look at everyone whose feelings you—I mean whose feelings have been hurt, and then think back on who left the Winter Workshop, we'll have a good list of suspects. Then we just ask them a few questions." She shrugs. "Maybe we'll get lucky."

We look at each other. "You never know," I say. "It could happen."

"Right! It could!" she says, looking very relieved. "Let's

see. I've been thinking about this, and it could be Kyle or Lauren."

"What did I do to them?"

"When you got Kyle's name-game card, remember? He told you he let you win it, but you didn't believe him. You thought he was bad at the game."

"I kind of remember it. Why Lauren?"

"You made her look bad in front of the whole class when we had to write those personal-history poems. You said writing was easy."

"Only because it is."

"You think just because something is easy for you, it's easy for everybody. But Lauren has to work hard at it and you embarrassed her."

"How do you know?"

"I was watching her face. Which you could do, too. It's not hard to notice that stuff."

"Maybe not for YOU," I say.

She smiles. "Okay, I get what you're saying. But you could try to be better at it."

We talk some more and add Hannah and Daisy and lots of other kids to the list. Ellie thinks pretty much everybody has a reason not to like me. I hope she's exaggerating.

When we're done, Ellie says, "That part didn't help as much as I thought it would. Let's figure out who had the chance to do it. We know Noah went to the bathroom, because he always does."

"Lauren had to go to her locker for something she forgot."

"Hannah came in late that day—right in the middle of the workshop, remember?"

"Yeah, the Winter Workshop Lady wasn't very happy about it."

"Okay, so that's our list. Noah, Lauren, and Hannah. There might be some others that we didn't see leave, but we can start with these."

"Wait! What about Arial? She likes to lie!"

"But she was in the workshop the whole time, right?"

"Oh, yeah."

"Then she's not a suspect. We can't put her on the list just because she likes to lie. Plus, she only lies for fun. She told me once that when she makes stuff up, it's like she's creating her own TV show and she gets to watch. I don't think Arial could do something like this." Ellie puts her arm around my shoulders and puts her head so close to mine that our ponytails bump into each other. "I don't think you could, either. I know you didn't take the globe." Which is the best thing she could say right then, and the thing my mom probably would have said, too, if I told her about all this.

Now all that's left is to ask the suspects if they did it.

We find Noah first. "If you took the globe, tell us now," I say. "Otherwise it will just be worse for you."

Ellie smiles at Noah and says, "Just a sec." Then she whispers in my ear, "I think this will go better if you let me do the talking."

"But that's not fair," I say. "It's my crime, so I should get to do the talking." Plus, if I'm not talking, I'm bored, which is the worst thing I can be.

"But they aren't mad at me, like they are at you," she whispers. And when she backs away from me, she nods and smiles, which means, *You can do this, Mary Margaret, because you want to catch the real robber.*

"Okay," I say.

Ellie turns back to Noah. "We're just asking the kids who left the Winter Workshop a few questions because maybe somebody saw something that will show Mary Margaret didn't do it."

Noah looks suspicious. "But she did do it."

"I did not!"

Ellie shoots me a look and then says to Noah, "Just tell us what you saw when you went to the bathroom. Did you see anyone in your classroom on your way by?"

Noah thinks for a second and then says, "Yes."

"Yes?" me and Ellie say together, all excited.

"When I walked by the door, I saw Mr. Mooney at his desk both times."

"Thanks, Noah," says Ellie. "That really helps." Ellie stretches the truth sometimes, but only to be nice. Even though I like almost every part of myself, sometimes I wish I could add in a part of Ellie. The part that is a natural at being nice.

"No problem," says Noah.

Recess is almost over by then, but lucky for us, Hannah and Lauren, our other two suspects, are swinging together. I remember to let Ellie talk.

She finds out they didn't do it.

The way she knows is because when Lauren went back

to her locker, she saw Hannah, who was late to school that day, come in and go to her locker, and Lauren went over there to ask why Hannah was late and they started talking about getting braces. And then they both walked to the Winter Workshop together.

As I stand in line next to Ellie, waiting to go in from recess, I think about how things are not looking very good for me. In a few more hours, it will be the end of the day and my life will be at the end of its rope, because that's when Mr. Mooney is going to call my mom and dad and tell them everything. I think about those World Famous Lipizzaner Stallions leaping through the air, leaping right out of my life.

What if we never find out who really stole the globe? Everybody will think I did it, forever and ever. I will be . . . *Robber Girl!* And every time something is missing, people will automatically think it's me that did it. What if even my mom and dad don't believe me and I end up being the bad one in my family, instead of Liza, who really IS the bad one? What if Santa wasn't watching when the globe got stolen? What if he thinks I'm guilty, like everybody else does? He's probably taking my presents out of the sleigh and putting in lumps of coal for me instead.

Thinking about it makes me madder and madder. And how mad I am gets all mixed up with being sad, too, which makes me want to yell and cry at the same second and that's hard to do. Except for if you're Liza, who is a rock star at that kind of thing. All I can do is shudder.

Ellie hugs me. "Don't worry."

"I won't," I say. And I mean it. Because all that shuddering shaked something up in me. It shaked up my quiet temper, which is the temper I get when something goes wrong and I decide it is my job to make it go right again. I grit my teeth together and say, "I won't, I won't, *I won't*," with every marching step I take up the sidewalk, into the school, down the hall, and all the way to my desk. Whoever did this to me is not going to get away with it.

I tell myself, it's not over until the old dog barks, which means things might be going bad for me but I can do something about it. My idea of my gut plus my brain didn't work that well, but neither did JT's motive plus opportunity, because that's what Ellie tried.

My dad always says that if something doesn't work, try, try again. I need another plan. So I do the first plan that pops into my head, because there isn't any time to wait for more plans to come along. I start asking people straight out, "Did you take Mr. Mooney's snow globe?" But I have to be sneaky about it because I think Mr. Mooney has about had it with me and this business.

Fortunately, Mr. Mooney knows that I have lots of ants in my pants, so my getting up to sharpen my pencil or look for a missing paper or to stretch myself is normal for me. All I have to do is add a little something to that routine.

On the way to sharpen my pencil, I stop at Ali's desk and stare into her eyes. "Did you take Mr. Mooney's globe?"

"No," she says.

"Why should I believe you?" I ask.

"Because I said it while looking you in the eye. And also because I never left the Winter Workshop."

"Good reason," I say.

After I pretend to sharpen my pencil, I stop at Arial/ Whopper Girl's desk. "Did you take the globe?"

She slowly writes 23 on her paper under the problem of 12 + 11. "No," she whispers without looking up. "But I did steal the Liberty Bell. I wore a hunting cap and sunglasses so the guards wouldn't see that I was just a kid and then I backed the truck in and loaded the bell on. It's in my closet. Don't tell anyone!"

I walk on. Snow globes are not glamorous enough for Whopper Girl.

I sit tight at my desk for a little while because I don't want to attract Mr. Mooney's eye. Lucky for me, Ethan walks by. "Ethan!" I hiss. And when he stops I whisper, "Did you take the globe?"

He raises his right hand, closes his eyes, and says, very serious, "I swear on my mother that I did not."

His eyes are closed, so that gets my suspicions up, but Ethan is mostly nice and polite. Way inside my heart I don't think he would drag his mother into a lie.

When I get up to s-t-r-e-t-c-h my arms, I stretch right over to Caleb's desk, because Jacob is already there and I can ask both of them at the same time. Except those two guys are clowns all the time. So I talk to them using their language. I hold up my hand like I'm showing the number four and put it in front of my face. "I'm in jail," I say.

"Ha-ha!" says Caleb.

"You are!" says Jacob.

"But," I say, "I'm innocent, so I shouldn't be in jail."

"That stinks," says Caleb.

"Tough luck," says Jacob.

"Right. Somebody should be in jail, but not me. Jacob, did you take the globe? Caleb? If you tell the truth, Santa will forgive you. If you lie, though . . . !"

Caleb says, "Ho-ho-ho! No-no-no!" and the whole time Jacob is shaking his head. So they didn't do it, either. And Caleb is making so much noise with his ho-ho-ho-ing that Mr. Mooney says, "Mary Margaret, I've been watching those ants run circles in your pants all afternoon. Time for them and you to cease and desist!"

Which means my research is over, because for the rest of the day he has his eyes on me almost every minute, even though he is also asking Daisy about her personal-history web, which is not done. And her poem, which isn't done, either. Mr. Mooney is yelling at her with words but yelling at me with his eyes. By the time we have to get ready to leave, Mr. Mooney has me and Daisy all frazzled up. When we get our coats on, I put my frazz on pause so I can ask more kids about the globe.

"Tristan!" I say very urgent. "Did you take the globe?"

Tristan looks at me like I'm crazy. "What would I want with a stupid globe?" he asks.

But before I can answer, the loudspeaker crackles and one of the fifth graders starts reading announcements. "This year's snowman contest will be on Friday. Also, don't forget to bring in your unwrapped presents for Toys for

Tots and leave them in Mr. Brunnik's room. Also, Tanner Stam, please report to the office. Tanner Stam."

And right then, even though the announcements are still going, a lightbulb of an idea comes out of my head. I remember that Daisy got called to the office when the rest of us were eating cookies in the cafeteria on the day the snow globe disappeared. Which means she had the chance to steal it without anyone seeing her.

This time I don't blab it out like I did when I thought McKenzie was the robber. This time I just slide up close to Daisy and say real low, "You took the globe."

"You wish," she says, without looking at me.

"I know."

"Well, wishing doesn't make it true."

"No," I say. "I mean I don't just wish you did. I know you did."

"You don't know anything, except how to be a Miss Look-at-Me," she says. Her face is getting splotchy with red spots. "And everybody's looking at you now." The more she talks, the splotchier she gets.

"Maybe I get carried away with myself and my ideas," I say, thinking about what Ellie said to me earlier on the playground. "But I don't steal."

"*I* do—but you can't prove it," she hisses, looking me straight in the eye.

"So you did take it?"

She looks at me like I'm dumb and says a little louder, "Yes, I took the stupid globe and I'm glad."

But just when she's saying the part about "I took the

stupid globe and I'm glad," the announcements end, and since everybody is quiet from listening to the announcements, everybody hears her. Including Mr. Mooney.

"Ah-HA!" I say, because that is what detectives always say on TV when they solve a crime, which I just did. And then I say it again, because it is fun to say. "Ah-HA!"

Mr. Mooney shoots a look my way that means, *Stop with the ah-has!*

"Daisy!" he says, very surprised. "It was you?"

Daisy doesn't say anything. Then she spouts out, "Only because she ruins everything. You know she does! She always has to be the big attraction and she can't stand it when someone else is. That stupid eyebrow trick and etcetera. I just got tired of her."

"Class dismissed," says Mr. Mooney.

I hang around because I'm pretty sure somebody owes me an apology. And etcetera.

"Mary Margaret, I'm sorry you got blamed for something you didn't do," he says. "That never feels good."

"No, it doesn't," I say, looking at Daisy because she is the one who owes me an apology, not Mr. Mooney.

He hands me my backpack. "Have a nice afternoon."

"Yeah, but—"

"That's all. I will see you tomorrow," he says. And then he says to Daisy, "We need to talk," and when they walk back to the classroom together, he puts his arm around her.

Which is way too nice when you are dealing with a hardened criminal, if you ask me. But nobody does ask me.

11. <u>Forgive?</u> Forget It!

All that afternoon, I feel very light and free. It's not even Christmas yet and I already got the thing that I most wanted—for everyone to know I didn't steal the globe. I don't even care very much that I had to do most of the work. Maybe Santa was resting up for the big day.

Now I can get back to the real meaning of Christmas—presents! I write out a new list, and that takes me a long time because I can't remember all the things I originally wanted, but I remember the list had four pages. So I watch TV for a while, because the commercials give me ideas for what I want. And pretty soon my list is even better than it was before, because now it's five pages long instead of four!

After I magnet my new list to the refrigerator door, I ask JT to help me add a light to the snow globe I made. The light will make the snow globe magical, which is what I want it to be for my mom. I think maybe some magic would cheer her up, even though she isn't getting what she wants most, which is more business. At first JT doesn't want to, but then I remind him that I helped him find the perfect gift for Natalie.

"No, you owed me for that, because you meddled in my social life," he says.

"But you were the one who asked me if Hannah had said anything about Natalie, remember?"

"But I didn't ask you to heart Natalie."

"I didn't even know I was hearting her! It was just a thingy-mabob and a three."

"But—oh, never mind."

While he is building a little platform for the snow globe, I tell him all about how things weren't looking very good for me at school all day, and how at the end of the day I rescued myself, and how tomorrow Mr. Mooney would probably make Daisy say she was sorry.

And JT doesn't tell me anything about his day, which is the way things go with us most of the time. I have an interesting life, so I have lots to say, but his life isn't that interesting, so he doesn't say much. Which works out good for me.

It seems like nobody has much to say that night, except for me and Liza. In fact, it's like my mom and dad are having a contest to see who can say the fewest words. Here is how their conversation at dinner goes.

Mom: I'm taking the van in tomorrow.
Dad: Okay.
Mom: Mary Margaret, the auto shop is close to school. Would you like me to pick you up?
Me: Okay.
(Nothing. For a long time.)

Dad: Pass the salad, please.

(Nothing for an even longer time.)

Liza: Mmm-bba.

Somebody has to talk. This kind of quiet must be bad for your health, because it is making me jittery.

"So!" I say, very bright. "You probably want to know how my day went because you always do. It was fantastic. Somebody took Mr. Mooney's snow globe—" And right here I stop and wait for my mom to say, "Oh, I love those things!" but she doesn't. She just nods. So I keep going. "And that person put it in my boot to make it look like I did it. But I didn't. So then I had to sniff out the person who did. And boy, that wasn't easy! At first I thought it was McKenzie, because she's never liked me and I've never liked her, either. But she was actually with the janitor that whole time, so it wasn't her. And then Ellie tried to help me figure out who it was, but she went too easy on kids, so no one confessed. But then at the last second I remembered Daisy got called down to the office during cookie time on Winter Workshop Day? Which means she had the chance to do it. And she confessed that she DID do it! I squeezed that confession out of her. She meant for only me to hear her say it, but because the announcements were done, she ended up telling the whole class. Boy, was I surprised, and you should have seen Mr. Mooney!"

"Hmmm," says my mom. "Sounds like it was just a misunderstanding."

HUH? I think. She must not be listening very well. "Mom, she did it *on purpose*."

"Still," she says. "Things happen sometimes and we just have to forgive and forget." She is talking to me but looking at my dad.

"Yes," says my dad, very mild. "Once there's an apology, it's good to just forgive and move on."

"Yeah, I bet I will get a big 'I'm sorry' tomorrow," I say.

"I should be so lucky," says my dad.

My mom doesn't say anything.

"Mmmm-wah-wah-WAAAH!" says Liza.

Which is the only part of our dinner that's normal.

Things aren't normal at school the next day, either. I bop into the room very happy that I am not the one in hot water. And very sure that Daisy will have to pay for what she did to me. Because when you do something bad, you get consequences. I think the very first consequence is that Daisy will apologize to me, so I give her lots of chances. I sit next to her during morning announcements. I squeeze in behind her when we line up for gym. But she never says anything to me. She doesn't even look at me. At recess, I finally just say it out, "Daisy, don't you want to say something to me?"

"No." She says it like she means it.

"You know, about stealing the globe and making it look like I did it when really it was you?"

"No."

Maybe she doesn't know about manners. "I just thought you might want to apologize to me."

"I'm not going to apologize because I'm not sorry. It would be wrong and a lie and etcetera."

This I don't get. "But you lied about the snow globe!" I say. "And that was wrong and a lie and etcetera!"

She crosses her arms and zips her lips and marches away.

I march, too—right back into the school and right back into our class, where Mr. Mooney is reading at his desk.

"Daisy says she isn't sorry and she won't apologize to me."

Mr. Mooney nods. "And you think she should be sorry."

"Yes."

"And that I should make her apologize to you."

"Yes. She *owes* me an apology," I say. "First, she stole the globe, which was wrong. Second, she made it look like I stole the globe, which I would never do! And third, she wasn't going to fess up—ever! She was going to let me take the blame. And she didn't even feel guilty about it!"

"I understand how you feel. But I can't make her apologize."

"Yes, you can. You're the teacher!"

"What I mean is, I can make her say the words, but I can't make her mean them. Is that what you want?"

I nod. "Yes. In front of the whole class."

"I'm afraid I can't do that. I just don't believe in forcing kids to be dishonest."

"But-but-but she's already been dishonest. She's good at it!"

Mr. Mooney smiles his sad smile. "I gave you a chance to prove you were innocent, and now I'm asking you to give Daisy a chance to get to the place where she feels sorry."

I think maybe she will need some help in that department. If Mr. Mooney's not going to help her, then I will have to do it myself. But I don't say so because Mr. Mooney might not see things exactly that way.

The rest of recess is productive, which means it's useful. And it's useful because by the time it's over, I have an idea. While everyone is still out in the hall taking off their coats and boots, I say, very loudly, "Who wants to be in my club?"

"I do!" says Ellie.

"Me, too!" says Arial.

McKenzie says, "I guess so."

"Well . . . what kind of club is it?" asks Caleb.

"A fun club," I say.

Jacob looks unsure. "What're you going to do in your club?"

I didn't think I'd have to know all this already. "Talk!" I say, because it is the first thing I think of. "And read! And talk about what we read."

Jacob rolls his eyes. "Boring."

I kick my brain into high gear. "And—and eat! Yes, we're going to eat! Brownies—with extra chocolate chips! And . . . potato chips with extra salt! And pop . . . with extra fizz!"

I sneak a look at Daisy and I can tell she is listening. My plan must be working so far.

Jacob and Caleb shrug. "Okay."

Tristan says no, though.

"Why not?" My idea will not work unless everyone goes with it.

"It doesn't sound fun."

"Well, what does sound fun?"

"Worm races are kind of cool," he says.

"And I like holes and trenches and hideouts," says Ethan.

"Okay," I say. "We can have all that stuff."

"So exactly what kind of club is it?" asks Lauren.

Everyone is staring at me again, just like they did when I pulled the snow globe out of my boot, but it feels different this time. This time it feels good. "It's the Everything Club because we'll do everything!" I say. "Find me later if you want to be in it. Pass it on."

I can tell everybody really does want to be in the club, but they are busy with desk work and they forget. So I help them. I remind them during lunch. And at recess. And when they still forget, I go from desk to desk, because I don't want them to miss the wonderful opportunity of being a member of the Everything Club. But I don't get all the way to Daisy's desk before Mr. Mooney starts making eyes at me, which means I should take my seat. Him and me have all kinds of codes, which is good because otherwise I think he would spend some quality time yelling at me.

But finally, at the end of the day, the thing I was hoping for happens.

Daisy asks me, "Are lots of kids signing up for your club?"

"Yup," I say.

"Is it full?"

"No."

"Can girls be in it?"

"Sure," I say.

"Do you have to be ten?"

"Nope. Just fourth grade."

"But only kids in Mr. Mooney's class?"

I nod.

"Only kids you're not mad at?"

"No, even kids I'm mad at can be in it. McKenzie's in it."

She doesn't say anything for a minute. Then she says, "Can I be in it?"

"No."

"But that's not fair! You let in fourth-grade girls. I'm a fourth-grade girl!"

"Any fourth-grade boy or girl without a history of crimes can be in the club."

"You can't just leave me out."

"Yes, I can. It's called the Every*thing* Club, not the Every*one* Club," I say.

Daisy's face starts getting splotchy again. "I am not sorry about the globe," she growls.

"I don't care," I say. Even though the only reason I'm having a club is to make her sorry for what she did to me.

"I'm even *more* not sorry about it than I was before you and your stupid club, which I don't want to be in!"

"You asked to be in it!"

"No, I asked if I could be in it. Even if you'd said yes, I would have said I didn't want to be."

And then she stomps away. Which is fine with me, because I have to get to the front of the school to meet my mom. When I get there, I don't see our van, so I stand outside the front door of the school in a place that's out of the wind. There are lots of people there waiting and talking, but I am busy keeping my eyes out for our van, so I can't look at them. In a minute, Arial/Whopper Girl yells from the other side of the sidewalk, "Hey, Mary Margaret! How come you're not taking the bus?"

"My mom is picking me up!" I yell back.

And then she yells, "Hey, why aren't you letting Daisy into the club?"

And then something gives me a little kick in the head. "Owww!" I say, turning to see what's attacking me. It's Liza and my mom. But it's Liza who kicked me. "Cut it out!" I say to Liza.

"Oh, Mary Margaret," says my mom. "She's just a baby. She didn't kick you on purpose."

Everyone thinks that just because Liza is a baby, she

doesn't know what she's doing. But she knows exactly what she's doing.

"Bye, Arial," I say, and I scoot right away from there.

"What's this about a club?" pants my mom. It's hard for her to keep up with me because Liza weighs her down.

"Oh, yeah. The Everything Club, that's what I'm calling it. We're going to do everything we like to do."

"But—what did Arial say? Something about Daisy not getting in."

"Mom, Arial is like the Internet. You can't believe everything she says."

"Hmmm," my mom says. "I'm not asking about everything. I'm asking about *this* thing."

Sometimes I wish my mom didn't know me so well. "I don't really want to talk about it right now," I say.

"Fair enough," she says.

"Was the van a lot of money to get fixed?"

"I don't know yet. It's taking them longer than they expected, so they gave me a loaner to come and pick you up."

"But I want to go home."

"It will just take a minute."

Which usually means it will take an hour, because my mom is terrible at guessing how much time stuff takes.

And guess what? I'm right about that. Our van isn't done when we get to the shop, so we have to haul Liza and her car seat into the little lobby and sit on these hard plastic chairs while we wait, which is boring. To entertain myself, I ruffle through all the things in my head, like Christmas and presents, but everything is in order there since everyone knows who really took the snow globe, thanks to me. Then I think about Daisy and I know she wants to be in the Everything Club, even if she won't admit it. And about how she says she's still not sorry she took the globe. Which still makes me mad. And that makes me think about my mom and dad.

"Are you and Dad still mad at each other?" I ask.

"I don't really want to talk about it right now," she says.

"You always say it can help to talk."

"Hmmm. I guess I do always say that. Let's make a deal. You talk about Daisy and your club and I'll talk about me and your father."

My plan is to just tell her a little bit. "I don't want liars and cheats in the club because it might be a bad influence."

"And that's the only reason you're excluding Daisy? What about Arial? You said she lies, but you're letting her in the club."

"That's different."

"Different how?"

"She doesn't lie about me."

"Like Daisy lied about you, in a way that hurt you." That's the thing about my mom. You think you're just going to tell her a little bit, but then she says something that makes everything else spill out of you. "Daisy did it on purpose. She sneaked into Mr. Mooney's room when no one else was there and she took the globe and she put it in my boot because she wanted everybody to think I took it because she thinks I'm annoying and I always have to be the center of attention. It's just so . . . mean! And WRONG. And she's not sorry! She's supposed to at least be sorry! She hasn't apologized or anything and Mr. Mooney isn't making her say she's sorry, which he should. He thinks she has to really BE sorry and then she will say it, and I just decided she needs some help feeling sorry, so that's all I'm doing with the club. She lied and because she lied she can't be in the club, so then she'll be sorry that she lied and *then* she'll apologize."

"I understand why you did it, Mary Margaret, but you can't make people feel a certain way. And it's not productive to try. You need to try to forgive her and move on."

When she says that, I think my ears must be broken. "I don't want to forgive her. Remember, *she* was mean to me."

"Well, just think about it," she says.

"No, thanks."

"It's important."

"Why?"

My mom looks at me and sighs. "Because character is the ticket."

"Why is it the ticket for me and not for her?"

My mom smiles and says, "Because she's not my daughter—and you are."

"You just said you can't make someone feel a way they don't feel. And I don't feel forgiveness."

That stops my mom, but only for a minute. "You're

right. I can't make you feel forgiveness any more than you can make Daisy feel sorry. But if you can't truly forgive her, then do the best you can. All I'm asking is that you make an effort."

"Why?"

"Because that's what's required of us. To show compassion for others. That's what makes the world a better place. Just think about it."

I think about it for about one second, while she is paying the mechanic lady, and here is what I decide. My mom needs to leave her thinking cap here at the repair shop, because it is not working right.

12. Staying Busy Is Hard Work

"Mom, no," JT complains. "I told you before, I'm too old for that stuff."

"Come on! I'm not asking you to sit on Santa's lap!" Mom says. "It's just caroling. You're never too old for that."

"Speak for yourself," JT says, and then he sniffles. "Besides, I feel like I'm coming down with a cold. You all could go and I could stay home with Liza."

"Nice try," she says, pulling our coats out of the front-hall closet. "But we're all going, just like we do the last weekend before Christmas every year. The Delaneys and McKays are expecting us to join our voices with theirs."

"And we're going to have fun, even if it kills us," growls my dad. Usually I would think he is joking, because he's a big jokester. But there hasn't been that much joking at my house lately.

"Who's the Grinch now?" my mom says very quiet to my dad. But I have supergood ears and I can hear just about anything when I want to.

My dad looks up and sees I'm listening. He doesn't answer her.

JT and I end up at the back of the group, which is okay with us. While we're walking to the Keatings' house after singing "Here Comes Santa Claus" for Jolene and her family, I trip on a chunk of ice and bump up against JT.

"Watch it!" he snaps.

Which means I have to bump him again, harder, because he's asking for it. Since we both have our big winter coats on, I just bounce right off him, like a bumper car, which makes me giggle. But then he bumps me back, hard, and I go flying like a snow angel right into the snowbank. I know he wants to pick a fight, but the snow is fluffy, and when I look up, I can see the stars and my mood is too twinkly to fight with him, even if he wants to.

I pat the snow beside me. "Come on! Make a snow angel with me," I say.

JT snorts. Right then my mom calls, "Are you coming?" Everybody else was almost to the Derrys' house. "Delta, Dakota, and Dallas are waiting!" The Derry triplets are twelve and they L-O-V-E love JT.

JT looks at me again then yells, "In a minute! We're making snow angels!" and sits down in the snow next to me and mumbles, "Anything is better than more girls."

I snowplow the snow with my arms and legs. "Did Natalie like her present?"

"Yeah, she liked it a lot. Thanks for helping me pick it out."

"Did you bust up with her?"

JT flops onto his back and says, "No."

"I don't get what the big deal is. If she knew, I bet she wouldn't even want to go with you. Because why would you want to be with someone who doesn't LIKE like you?"

JT doesn't say anything.

"I bet you wish you were nine," I say. "Everybody knows who likes each other. For example, Caleb and Jacob. And everybody knows who doesn't like each other. For example me and McKenzie. Nobody pretends to like somebody they don't."

"Being thirteen is more complicated," JT says. "And things only really got bad when you hearted Natalie."

"Sorry," I say. Because I really am sorry. Unlike some people I know, whose name begins with *D* and ends with *Y* and has an *A-I-S* in the middle.

After church the next day, presents are on my mind, probably because the minister kept talking about "the biggest gift of all," which is just another word for *present*. So I have to work hard at keeping myself busy to keep my mind off the presents in the house that are still wanting me to come to them. First I stare at myself in the bathroom mirror and flick the lights on and off very fast and watch the black center of my eyeball shrink from big to little. But after a while that gives me a headache.

Next I redecorate the tree. I take off the six red velvet ribbons that hang from the star on the top of our tree all the way down to the bottom branches. Then I take off the four white velvet ones. I move all the ornaments hanging around the bottom half of the tree to the top half. Then I run a red ribbon around the very bottom of the tree, and then a white ribbon just above the red, then another red and another white, so it looks like the tree is wearing a red-and-white-striped skirt. Then I take all the tinsel off the tree and hang it along the bottom, so it looks like the skirt has a glittery fringe. And that leads to my next bright idea, which is to run upstairs and cut sleeves off an old sweatshirt and stuff the sleeves full of wadded-up toilet paper. I stick one sleeve on each side of the tree, so the tree looks like it has real arms. Then I wad up more toilet paper, which I have to round up from all the bathrooms because we are almost out, and stuff it into a white pillowcase.

Because quite a while ago I learned the lesson about not markering on pillowcases or towels or anything this family might use, I cut up some black construction paper into eyes and eyelashes and even eyebrows, because I've decided that faces do look better with both eyebrows. I tape those onto the stuffed pillowcase, along with red construction-paper lips. *Ta-da!* I think, holding it up. A head for the tree.

I open the cleaning closet to get the stepladder and inside I find my lucky pig ear. After snatching it up, I shove it into my pocket, because who knows when I'll need that thing next? From the top of the stepladder, I can reach the star at the top of the tree. I take it off and put on the head. I climb down and turn on the lights, which have stayed right where they were. I am not to rearrange the lights. Or even touch them. Ever. That was another lesson I learned the hard way when I was little, according to my dad. But I don't remember how I learned it, and whenever I ask him about it, he just puts his head in his hands.

I back away so I can get a better look at my creation, which is a cross between a snowman and a Christmas tree. A Christmas-Man, wearing a skirt.

I clap for myself because it is the best tree ever. Very original and stylish. It will be a new trend, and next year everyone will decorate their trees this way, I bet.

My mom comes in to see what all my noises are about. "That's quite something," she says.

"I know!" I say, very excited. "And I did it all on my own. It's a Christmas-Man in a skirt."

"I can see the skirt, and the shirt of ornaments, and the arms and head are made of . . . ?"

"Toilet paper," I say. "And oh, by the way, we need more of that from the grocery store."

"Why isn't it a Christmas-Lady?"

I shrug. "It just isn't. It's a Christmas-Man in a skirt. I made it up and I get to decide. Where's Dad? I want to show him."

"Out with Liza."

"Ohhhh, out doing Christmas secrets?" I wink as good as I can.

"He didn't tell me," she says, not at all playful back. Her Christmas cheer must have gone on vacation. "Have you thought any more about forgiving Daisy?"

"Nope," I say. "Because I am not going down that path."

"I think you should reconsider," she says, moving an angel ornament to another branch.

I move the angel ornament back to where it was. "That wouldn't be very productive."

"No?"

"No."

"Then let me put it this way. Down that path, the Lipizzaners lie."

"You mean the World Famous Lipizzaner Stallions Show?"

She nods.

"So if I don't forgive Daisy, I won't be able to go to the show? But that's not fair! She's not sorry!"

"Mary Margaret, listen. I know she's not sorry and you can't make her be. And I can't force you to forgive her. I'm just asking that you take a step in that direction. Let her know you haven't given up on her just because she made one bad choice. We've all made bad choices."

Right then my dad calls on the phone. My mom's side of the conversation is very short, like hello–yes–yes–no–good-bye. Which makes me remember that my mom actually never did tell me why she and Dad are not talking, after I told her all about the Everything Club.

"Is that why you're mad at Dad—because he made a bad choice?" I ask after she hangs up.

"Don't change the subject," she says. "This is about you and about understanding we all make bad choices. And even when someone does—"

"You don't cross them off your list," I say, hoping to end this part of our little talk.

"That's right. Just do what you can to forgive her, in your own unique way. That's all I'm asking."

"And if I find a way to show I'm not giving up on her, *then* I'll be able to go to the World Famous Lipizzaner Stallions Show?" Because that's all I really want to know.

She laughs a little. "Yes."

"Okay. I'll try in my own way, but only because you're making me."

"I can live with that," she says.

"But this trying-to-forgive stuff is only until I grow up, right? And then I can be like you and Dad and decide whether I even want to try."

My mom nods slowly and then her face changes, like she's suddenly thought of something new. "That's right," she says. "Then it will be completely up to you." And even though our little talk was not that much of a happiness for me, she must not see it that way, because right then she winks at me and says, "By then, I bet you'll do it without even thinking." Which makes me feel good. It also makes me wonder if my mom knows me very well, because so far forgiveness is not my favorite thing. Or even number ten on that list.

"JT!" my mom says suddenly. "I'll take JT with me!"

"With you where?"

"Shopping. I mean out."

"What about me?"

"You can stay here. Dad will be back in less than half an hour."

"No, thanks," I say, because that would be breaking the rule I made for myself about not being in the house alone for even a few minutes.

"What? You hate to shop!"

"I hate to be here alone right now worse," I say.

"I'm sorry, but you can't come along this time. We're going to be Christmas shopping—for you!"

This is a problem. If I stay, I'll find out about my Christmas presents. If I go, I'll find out about a new Christmas present. But then the answer pops into my head just like answers do sometimes. "I'll wait in the car. I'll bring a book to read and I will wait in the car for you and JT."

My mom looks at me like I'm a mystery. Then she throws up her hands and says, "All right. So be it. But no snooping through bags in the car."

That makes me laugh on the inside, but I don't let the laugh out.

There are a bunch of stores in the strip mall, so I don't even know what kind of thing Mom is buying, and JT isn't very happy Mom dragged him along.

"It will only take a minute," she says. "I know exactly what I'm after."

"Then why do you need me?" JT grumps.

"Because I don't know exactly exactly, and that's where you are going to help me."

JT sighs and follows her across the parking lot and

down a sidewalk. The sun shining through the windows keeps the inside of the van warm and I disappear into my book, very happy with the way I solved this problem.

I am in the middle of a good part, when the kids in the story are on the porch of this house they think might be haunted and one kid has dared another to go in and the first kid edges up to the door but before he can even answer the door opens and something snatches him off his feet and—

Rap-rap-rap!

"Wah!" I yelp, jolting straight up out of my seat. Fortunately, it's just Taylor knocking on the window of the van and not a ghost.

"Sorry!" she says through the glass. "I didn't mean to scare you."

I am not supposed to open the door for strangers, but JT knows Taylor and Taylor has been to our house, so I decide she's not a stranger and I open the door.

"Sorry," she says again. "Is JT with you?"

"He's in a store with my mom, but I don't know which one."

"Can you give him a message? Just tell him that he and Natalie aren't going together anymore."

"They're not? What happened?"

Taylor shrugs. "I think she kind of freaked about getting him the perfect present. She said something about Hannah was supposed to help her but didn't and then JT got her something she really wanted. She cracked under the pressure. I was going to IM JT later, but when I saw you here, I thought I'd just tell you now."

"Okay, I'll tell him," I say.

After she leaves, I watch shoppers lug their bags through the slushy parking lot and load them into trunks. I decide Santa's way is better than all this shopping. Elves make the toys, wrap the toys (although Ellie's presents from Santa come unwrapped, so I guess it depends on where you live), load them into a sleigh, and then Santa delivers presents—right to your tree. You just have to make sure the tree is the kind with no lower branches so there's room for the presents.

Just then I see JT and my mom come around the corner. I know I should put my hands over my eyes so I won't see the name of the store on the bag, but I don't have much practice yet at not looking at clues that are right in front of my eyes without any warning. So I stretch my neck and look and look and look. Neither of them is even carrying a bag.

I am not supposed to notice, so when they get in the van, I act all *la-di-da*, like I have forgotten that they were shopping for a present for me.

JT rolls his eyes at my little act. "You're in luck, Mary Christmas. They were fresh out of lumps of coal, so Mom's going to have to find something else."

"Ha-ha," I say.

"I guess I could call around and see if anyone else has them," my mom says, but it's more like she's talking to herself than to us.

"Hey, JT, I've got great news for you!" I say. "You and

Natalie are not going together anymore! Taylor told me while you were shopping."

That snaps my mom right up to attention. "You had a girlfriend?"

"No, just this girl I was going with but now I'm not. End of story."

Except that there's something I need to add to the story. "You want to know why? It's because I wouldn't tell Hannah what to buy you for Christmas."

"The girl's name was Hannah?" asks my mom.

"No!" JT and I both say.

"Hannah is Natalie's sister," I explain, very helpful. "And I was supposed to give her the present I bought for JT."

"You were?" asks JT.

"Yes, but then I didn't because she went back on the deal we made."

"What deal?" asks JT.

"It doesn't matter anymore," I say, hoping he'll drop that subject. I don't want to have to explain about the name game in front of my mom. "Anyway, Natalie freaked—that's what Taylor said—and decided they weren't going together anymore."

"Oh, JT," says my mom, very sweet. "I'm sorry. Girls that age can be so fickle."

"Mom, really, I don't care," says JT. "I'm *glad*."

Mom doesn't even hear that, though, because right away she says, "As soon as we get home, we can talk it all out over a cup of hot cocoa."

"There is nothing to talk out," JT groans. "And I don't want hot cocoa."

But Mom just nods and we both know she's not going to change her mind.

Which is why, when we get out of the van back at home, JT growls low so Mom can't hear, "Thanks a lot, Mary Blabbermouth."

"But did you notice that it was me who got you out of the whole girl thing?" I ask.

"It was also you who got me into—oh, never mind," he says.

Sometimes the only way to win an argument with JT is to hang in there until he gives up first. And I've had a lot of practice at that.

13. Where I Do the Right Thing—Again

The next few days at school go by S——L——O——W, because that is what happens when you're waiting for something fun, which Christmas is. The days before holiday break are the slowest of all. I don't even have the Everything Club to spark things up because my mom said I had to let Daisy be in it, and if I didn't, she would find out. Being related to Santa must mean that she has some of his powers. Nothing very interesting happens, except me and Daisy flounce by each other a lot. She flounces to let me know she's still not sorry. I flounce because I did the right thing and she did the wrong thing. Also because flouncing is fun.

But then I make a problem for myself by flouncing at home.

"Mary Margaret," says my mom. "I can tell by how happy you are that you must have found a way to reconcile with Daisy. I would love to hear about it."

Oh, that, I think to myself. I wonder why my mom forgets stuff I want her to remember and remembers all the things I wish she'd forget. "Well," I say, "I'm not ready to talk about it yet." Which is true because I haven't actually found a way to make up with Daisy.

"That's fine," she says, very easy. "But tomorrow is your last chance before the holiday break to do it. So you might want to move it up on your priority list."

"Which means?"

"Basically, do it—or else."

"Just wanted to make sure."

I already know that "or else" equals not going to the World Famous Lipizzaner Stallions Show. So I don't have to ask about that.

I stop with the flouncing and clomp to my room. Even though my mom's not making me forgive Daisy (because she can't make me, no one can), I don't really get why I even have to try. After all, Daisy's not asking me to.

I flop down on my bed, because it's easier for the blood to get to my brain that way and I need my brain to do some good desk work to solve this problem. My dad always says I should try to look at problems in lots of ways. If I look at *forgiveness* in a different way . . . like backwards! Senevigrof. And if I say *forgiveness* backwards, it probably means the opposite of forgiveness, which works out good for me. I could say with zest, "Daisy, I senevigrof you!" because it would actually mean I *don't* forgive her. And that is the truth.

Whispering *senevigrof, senevigrof, senevigrof* to the beat of my hooves, I trot out of my room like a proud horse, because I have solved my problem.

"Mom," I say when I find her changing Liza's diaper.

"You don't have to think about the 'or else' anymore!"

"No?" she says.

"No, because I am doing what I can to forgive Daisy, just like you told me. I am going to say to her tomorrow, 'Daisy, I evigrof you.' Dad always says to look at problems in a different way, so I looked at it backwards."

"I can see you're very excited about your idea, which didn't even take you long to come up with. Did you say *ennigrof*?

"No, e-vig-rof."

"Which is *forgive* backwards," she says.

"Mmm-hmmm," I say, holding my breath, hoping she will like my idea.

"Mmm-mmmm-mmm," goes Liza.

Mom wraps the used diaper up into a neat little ball and throws it in the trash. She picks Liza up and hands her to me. I make a face.

"Just until I wash my hands," she says.

Lugging Liza, I follow her into the bathroom so I can watch her think. She is an overachiever at hand washing.

"Well?" I say. "What do you think?"

She dries her hands slowly and takes Liza from me. "What I think is nice try, but no dice. I suspect from your enthusiasm that *evigrof* means you don't forgive her. You're dodging, Mary Margaret."

"But she won't know that!"

"I love you too much to argue with you," she says.

Thinking how much I hate it when she says that, I plod back to my room, my spirit twisted and broken.

I flop onto my bed again, then decide I need to make it even easier for my blood to get to my brain. So I stand on my head. I'm very good at standing on my head on the floor, so I think I can probably do it on my bed. While I'm up there, I think up a poem about forgiving.

Ode to Daisy
You put the globe
In my boot
To make it look
Like my loot
You deserve to be in jail
And go to the bathroom
In a pail.

That makes me giggle, which makes me fall out of my headstand and onto my back.

I love to laugh, so I let myself laugh for a long time. Plus, it's hard to stop laughing when you are on your back. I don't know why.

Once all my laughs are out, though, I remember that I still have a problem.

I twizzle my head to look at my bookshelf, which is piled high with books. On top of the books is my favorite red sweater. On top of the sweater is an old ant farm, with no ants. I used to have ants, but that is another story. I twizzle my head the other way to look at my dresser. I cannot actually see my dresser, but I know it is there, under the blanket that I laid over it so I could display my rock and bone collection, which is a very interesting collection if you like rocks and bones.

Something is prickling my bum. I reach under there and pull out a horse chestnut, which is a very prickly thing. My dad always says my room is so messy it's dangerous, and now I know what he means. I think maybe sometime I should clean it. But the last time I cleaned it, it was too much work. I looked at it and said, "I will never be able to get this whole room clean." And my dad said, "Break it into smaller chunks. First, just clean up the bookcase. Then pick up the floor. Chunks, okay? I'll help you." So we chunked my room, like he said. But it was still a lot of work.

Then my brain skips from chunking my room to Daisy. And so those two things bang together in my head, and since chunking worked on the problem of cleaning my room, I decide to try to chunk my forgiveness problem.

I get out a piece of paper and write down *FORGIVNES*. Then I chunk it. *FOR-GIV-NES*.

I say it slow. Then I say it without looking at the word. Then I hop around the room and sing it. And that's when my brain gives me the answer. Because when you hop around the room singing FOR-GIV-NES in a high voice, it sounds like four-gift-es. Four gifts! I will give Daisy four gifts. I will four gift her.

One of the things I like about me is that I never run out of ideas. They just bing-bing-bing right out of me. And this one's a good one.

"I know how to forgive Daisy," I tell my mom, who's in the kitchen making dinner. Since she doesn't have any parties to plan, she cooks a lot.

"Good. You can explain it to me while you make the salad. Lettuce is in the fridge. You can throw in some cherry tomatoes and grated cheese."

While I'm washing the lettuce, I tell my mom all about how I was lying on my bed, waiting for an idea, but then how I stood on my head on the bed and then fell off and laughed a lot, and she says, "Mmm-hmm, mmm-hmmm," the whole time. And then I tell her about lying on my floor and looking around at my messy room and remembering about how Dad said to chunk jobs. And then I tell her how I chunked *forgiveness* so that now I will four gift Daisy. At the end of all that, I smile very big.

She hands me the cherry tomatoes and says, "Hmmmm."

"You said I could do it my own way and that I should just try, right?"

"That's right," she says. "But you didn't try very hard last time."

"But I am now," I say. "And I honestly think it's the best I can do on this forgiveness thing."

My mom is quiet for a minute and then says, "All right. I think that could work."

"Yay!" I shout, throwing cherry tomatoes in the air. And then it rains down cherry tomatoes on us. And my mom, who has been cranky a lot lately, smiles—and then ducks.

At first, she wants to know what presents I'll be giving Daisy. But I talk and talk and talk, which wears her ears out. Also I say this is something I can do on my own. It's something I want to do on my own. My mom is very big on us learning to do things on our own.

"You're really willing to spend your own money on this?"

"Oh, no," I say. "It won't take any money. I'll give her stuff I already have."

"I suppose it would be awkward if you showed up with four real gifts and she had nothing for you. That might make things worse."

"So you'll let me do my idea?" Because I'm busy with the tomatoes, I can't cross my fingers, so I cross my legs instead for good luck.

Finally, she says very straight out at me, "All right. I trust you'll pick the gifts for a reason, and that you'll make sure things are better between you and Daisy after you four gift her than they are now."

I nod, thinking that she never has to see what I give Daisy because I'll give the things to Daisy at school tomorrow. And they'll be old things I don't want anymore.

It's a good plan until my mom says, "I'll drive you and the four gifts to Daisy's house tomorrow."

"That's okay. I'll see her at school."

"No, I don't mind driving you. That way you don't have to worry about forgetting or losing the presents or not having enough time," she says. "It's all settled."

———

Daisy's dog bounds out to greet us as soon as we pull in the driveway. I'm still annoyed that my mother is making me do this, but seeing a cheerful dog all full of spirit is a happiness even when you don't want to feel happy.

I clump up to the door and ring the bell. My mom is right behind me, even though I tell her I can do it all by myself.

"It would be rude of me to wait in the car," she says. But I'm pretty sure she's mostly doing it because she wants to see the presents. And I can't be too mad about that, since presents are very attractive things that are hard to resist.

Daisy is surprised to see me, and I know from the eyebrow my mom raises at me that my mom is surprised Daisy is surprised. A lady comes to the door and invites us in. She says she's Daisy's nanny. I almost laugh out loud because *nanny* is a funny word. If you say it over and over fast, it makes a sound like a sick goat. And then Daisy's mom comes to the door, too, and Mom introduces us all over again.

But then Daisy's mom's cell phone rings and she says, "I'm very sorry but I have to take this call. It's a client."

And my mom smiles and says, "I understand how that is."

As Daisy's mom walks away she calls back over her shoulder, "What would we ever do without cell phones?" and Daisy rolls her eyes.

So then it's just Mom and me standing there with Daisy and her nanny.

My mom elbows me to remind me why I'm there, but I have to get warmed up before I give Daisy the things I brought. "So that's your mom," I say. "Is your dad here?"

Daisy shakes her head. "Not right now."

"Daisy's parents are separated," says the nanny. "She's going to see him after Christmas. They're going skiing together, aren't you, sweetie?"

"Yeah," says Daisy.

"That sounds wonderful," says my mom.

I don't think it sounds wonderful at all. I have a good imagination, but I can't picture my parents not living together, even if they do fight sometimes. I can't picture Christmas morning with just my mom, or just my dad. Although, you'd probably get twice as many presents, and that would be cool, so maybe . . . no, I wouldn't trade that even for more presents.

Daisy doesn't look like she thinks it's wonderful, either. "I hate to ski."

"Oh, sweetie," says her nanny. "You haven't even tried it."

She rolls her eyes again. "I said I hate it."

She says it like she hates more than just skiing. She says it like she hates a whole bunch of things, maybe even everything.

"I brought you four gifts," I blurt out, thinking that presents might be one thing Daisy doesn't hate. I don't say, "I am four gifting you," because I don't want her to think I'm forgiving her. "They aren't new, but I wanted you to have them."

Daisy holds the bag way out in front of her, like she's worried the presents are booby traps. "You hate me."

"That's an awfully strong word," my mom says. "I don't think she hates you, do you, Mary Margaret?"

"No," I say, because there aren't very many things I hate, besides being bored.

"But you're mad at me," Daisy says. "Why do you want to give me presents?"

I don't want to. My mom is making me. "Oh, just because," I say. So I can go to the World Famous Lipizzaner Stallions Show, I think to myself. So my mother will stop bugging me. So I can get back to my Christmas and my presents.

Daisy leans over and whispers in my ear, "I'm still not sorry."

Which is why I'm still not forgiving, I think to myself.

Then she looks up at her nanny. "Should I open them now?"

"I think that would be polite," she says.

So Daisy unwraps the first gift. My mom leans in, very interested.

"Oh!" says Daisy, pulling off the paper. "Sunglasses."

"Actually, they're spy glasses. When you wear them, you can see stuff that's happening behind you." They are cool, but whenever I tried to use them, they gave me a headache. "They're good if you want to lead a life of crime."

My mom pokes me, which means I should watch it. Or else.

The second present is a brand-new dictionary that my aunt Wendie gave me, but that I forgot about after it got lost in my room. That is the problem with messy rooms. They make things disappear. Sometimes a messy room will spit something up again, sometimes it won't. The dictionary got spit up just in time for this.

I know my mom won't be happy about me giving it away, since someone gave it to me as a present, so before Daisy can say anything, I say, "Because I thought learning new words . . ." But then I zip my lip up so the end of the sentence can't come out. Because the end of it is, "would be good because maybe you would use them instead of always saying *etcetera.*"

Daisy rubs her hand over the cover like she really likes it. I think about how it really is a nice dictionary. I kind of wish I'd kept it for myself.

The third present is a pink bandanna with bones and balls and squirrels. I bought it a while ago for the dog I planned to get. But I don't still don't have a dog, and Daisy does, so that's why I'm giving it to her.

Right away she ties it onto *her own head.*

"Umm," I says, "that's actually—"

"I love it!" she says. "Pink is my favorite color."

I shrug. Now my mom is smiling at me, so things must be going better for me.

"Thanks for all this," Daisy says, wadding up all the paper and stuffing it into the bag.

"Isn't there one more?" my mom asks.

Rats! I think. The truth is that there wasn't anything

else of mine I wanted to give up, especially to Daisy. I was hoping my mom wouldn't notice, but hoping didn't work out that well. My mom's looking at me and I can tell she's thinking that we agreed on four gifting, not three gifting, and I need to come up with number four fast like a bunny, quick like a rabbit.

"Can I use your bathroom?" I ask suddenly.

My mom frowns at me, very suspicious, but the nanny nods and points me in the right direction. While I'm in there, I tap my brain for ideas and it gives me two. One is that I could offer to let Daisy into the Everything Club. But that isn't even a real club. I only made it up to make Daisy feel sorry. My other idea is to give her my candy-machine dollar that's wadded up along with some other important things in my pocket. Yanking it out, I think how hard it will be not to be able to buy Red Hots and Super Sour Balls for another whole week, but I have to do it.

Walking back, I notice how big Daisy's house is—so big she might be rich. I walk past three Christmas trees, each one decorated differently. But even with all those trees, the hallway feels kind of empty. Even with all those trees plus the nanny and a dog and a mom, it doesn't feel exactly happy there.

"Well?" my mom says, when I'm beside her again.

I'm ready to give Daisy the dollar and get out of there, but then it hits me she doesn't need money. I reach into my pocket for the thing she *does* need.

My mom sees what I'm doing and gasps. "Are you sure?" she asks. "You really want to part with that?"

I nod. And before I can change my mind, I hand over my lucky pig ear to Daisy. "This present is the best of all of them," I say.

"Ewwww," she says, holding it by the tip.

I think about grabbing back my pig ear and making a run for it, since she doesn't have any respect for it.

But then I think about trying to be without my dad on Christmas morning and how I'd miss the way he shuffles in with his camera. I'd miss how he just sits there, kind of slumpy for a while, his eyes just slits because he hasn't even had a sip of coffee yet. I'd miss our Christmas-morning tradition where he picks me up and carries me in his arms like I'm a princess or a present, even, and then he tells me I *am* a present—one of the three best he's ever gotten. (I used to be one of the best two, until Liza barged in on that.) I'd even miss his pokey-outey hair. I think about how our family would seem all wrong without him, like a Christmas tree after you take off all the decorations and it just stands there all bare and sad. Our family would be empty, even if all the rest of us—me and JT and Eliza and my mom—were still in the family.

And that's why I don't grab the ear and run. Instead, I say to her, "It's a pig ear. It's not real, but it is really lucky, if you stroke it just right. Like this, with your thumb." I show her how to do it from the pointy tip all the way down the outside edge. "And then you have to start at the tip again."

Daisy looks a little unsure, like maybe I'm playing a trick on her.

"It's one of Mary Margaret's most treasured possessions," my mom says. "She hasn't ever even let her brother borrow it."

JT has never asked, but I know what my mom is doing. She's helping me and Daisy out.

"Really?" Daisy asks. "And you're giving it to me?"

I think about how I didn't even have that pig ear when I figured out that Daisy had framed me. "I've gotten better about being lucky all on my own," I say.

Daisy's eyes get bright, like she could maybe cry. I look to see if her nanny is pinching her like my mom sometimes pinches me when she wants me to pay attention, but nope. They are real tears. And then she says, very quiet, "I'm sorry for, you know, what happened in school and etcetera. I was so mad at you and the way you have to be in the middle of things . . ."

"That's okay," I say. The center of me used to feel like a frozen stick of butter whenever I thought of Daisy. But now it feels thawed out. Not completely soft, but soft enough to spread on warm toast. And that's how I know Daisy and I are okay enough, even if we aren't 100 percent okay. Someday we might be 100 percent, though, if I train myself to forget about what she did to me the way I trained myself to forget everyone's middle name after the name game was over. It probably wouldn't be very hard.

My mom grins, not in an "I told you so" way, but just like she can tell that things are a little better between me and Daisy.

Daisy's mom wiggles back into the hallway in her high heels. "I'm so sorry," she says again.

"That's all right," says my mom. "Mary Margaret just wanted to drop a few things off for Daisy, and she's done that, so we'll be on our way. Nice meeting you. Have a wonderful holiday."

"It will be a quiet one for us, unfortunately."

"Oh?" says my mom.

"I wanted to throw a fabulous New Year's Eve party— you know, to cheer the year up a bit—but I don't think I could ever get a caterer now."

My mom and I look at each other. I nod, like "do it!"

She turns to Daisy's mom. "I may be able to help you," she says, reaching into her purse and pulling out a card. "I have a party-planning business, and I bet I could still find you a caterer for New Year's Eve. I know a lot of people in the business."

As we walk down the sidewalk to the van, Mom says to me, "Well! You never know!"

She's right. Because even when you think you know things like you'll never like someone even a teeny tiny bit because she did something super-mean to you . . . well, you don't *know* know. You know?

14. Giving Thanks

It's weird how you can't wait for Christmas and it takes forever to get here and then—BANG! It's over. Luckily, there's still the World Famous Lipizzaner Stallions Show to look forward to, right after New Year's Day.

For now, though, there are lots of thank-you notes to write, which Mom tells me I should do while she makes phone calls for Daisy's mom's party. I strap on the Christmas eye patch JT gave me (it has Rudolph on it and his red nose blinks off and on for REAL) and get to work. I write my favorite thank-you note last.

Dear Santa,

Thanks for bringing me the Breyer horses. They are exactly what I wanted and the barn, too. And the CD. I like the handcuffs pretty well (even though they are the plastic ones and not REAL). Also, I know it's not your fault that I didn't get a puppy. I know you really wanted to bring me one but Dad told you not to because of his allergies. I'm glad you wrote in your letter that your sleigh wasn't big enough to fit everything on my list, even though I was very good this year. Maybe you should start saving so you can buy a bigger sleigh for next year. That's what I would do if I were you.

I think it's neat you were able to get us a hm-hm-hm, which was actually a Tuo-Duo game system for our TV, because those things were impossible to get! I don't know how you did that, but it sure made Dad smile (mostly at Mom)—and that present wasn't even for him.

Have a great year up there at the North Pole. In case you want a head start on next year's work, here are a few things I'd like . . . JUST KIDDING. I always wait until St. Patrick's Day to start my Christmas list for next year because that is one lucky day.

XO and gotta go!

Mary Margaret

After I'm done, I tape the thank-you note to the refrigerator, right where Santa's sure to see it when he goes on his "thank-you note" trip through all the houses. I smile and think about how me and Santa are on the same side when it comes to presents. We both live for them! I think about how happy presents make me and everyone else. Presents are what made things okay between me and Daisy, and maybe my—I mean *her*—lucky pig ear will be lucky enough that her mom and dad stop being separated. The perfect present got JT what he wanted, which was to be done with the whole girl thing. My mom loved the present I gave her—the snow globe, which is the Nativity scene of our family. I showed her how, when you shake us up, we all float around but eventually we end up back at home, and she cried and said, "This is what Christmas is all about."

Which just goes to show that the true meaning of Christmas really is presents, just like I thought all along.